'I did have hallucinations, but did they harm anyone? Whom did they harm, that's what I'd like to know?'

ANTON CHEKHOV
Born 1860, Taganrog, Russian Empire
Died 1904, Badenweiler, German Empire

'A Nervous Breakdown' was first published in 1889; 'The
Black Monk' in 1894; and 'Anna Round the Neck' in 1895.
This selection has been taken from three volumes of
Chekhov's short stories published in Penguin Classics.

CHEKHOV IN PENGUIN CLASSICS
The Steppe and Other Stories, 1887–1891
Ward No. 6 and Other Stories, 1892–1895
The Lady with the Little Dog and Other Stories, 1896–1904
The Shooting Party
Plays
A Life in Letters
Gooseberries

ANTON CHEKHOV

A Nervous Breakdown

Translated by
Ronald Wilks

PENGUIN BOOKS

PENGUIN CLASSICS

UK | USA | Canada | Ireland | Australia
India | New Zealand | South Africa

Penguin Classics is part of the Penguin Random House group of companies
whose addresses can be found at global.penguinrandomhouse.com.

This selection first published in Penguin Classics 2016
001

Set in 9.5/13 pt Baskerville 10 Pro
Typeset by Jouve (UK), Milton Keynes
Printed in Great Britain by Clays Ltd, St Ives plc

A CIP catalogue record for this book is available from the British Library

ISBN: 978-0-241-25178-2

www.greenpenguin.co.uk

Contents

A Nervous Breakdown

One evening a medical student called Mayer, and Ryb-
nikov, a pupil at the Moscow Institute of Painting,
Sculpture and Architecture, called on their law-student
friend Vasilyev and invited him to pay a visit to S— Street
with them. Vasilyev took a long time to make up his mind
but finally put his coat on and went off with them.

He knew of fallen women only by hearsay and from
books, and he had never been in their houses. He knew that
there were immoral women forced to sell their honour for
money under pressure of circumstances – environment,
poor upbringing, poverty and so on. These women knew
nothing of pure love, had no children, no legal rights.
Their mothers and sisters mourned them as if they were
dead, science treated them as an evil and men spoke to
them with contempt. But for all this they had not lost the
image and likeness of God. All of them acknowledged
their sin and hoped to be saved – and the paths to salvation open to them were innumerable. It is true that society
does not forgive people their past, but Mary Magdalene

is no lower than other saints in the sight of God. Whenever Vasilyev happened to recognize a prostitute in the street from her dress or manner, or whenever he saw a picture of one in a humorous paper, he always remembered a story that he had once read somewhere: a certain pure and self-less young man falls in love with a prostitute and asks her to become his wife, but she considers herself unworthy of such happiness and poisons herself.

Vasilyev lived in one of the side-streets leading off the Tver Boulevard. It was about eleven o'clock when he left the house with his friends. The first winter snow had only just begun to fall and the whole of nature was held captive by this fresh snow. The air smelt of snow; snow softly crunched underfoot; the ground, roofs, trees, boulevard benches – all was soft, white and new, and the houses looked quite different from the day before. The lamps shone more brightly, the air was clearer and the clatter of carriages was muffled. And one's sensations became just like the touch of white, new, fluffy snow in that fresh, light frosty air.

> 'Unwilling to these sad shores
> A mysterious force is drawing me'

sang the medical student in a pleasant tenor.

> 'See the windmill now in ruins'

the art student joined in.

> 'See the windmill now in ruins'

repeated the medical student, raising his eyebrows and sadly shaking his head.

He stopped singing for a moment, rubbed his forehead as he tried to recall the words, then he sang so loudly, so well that passers-by looked round at him.

'Here once I did meet light-hearted love, as free as myself.'

The three entered a restaurant and each drank two glasses of vodka at the bar without taking their coats off. Before they swallowed the second, Vasilyev noticed a piece of cork in his, raised the glass to his eyes and gazed at it for a long time, blinking shortsightedly. His expression appeared strange to the medical student.

'Why are you staring like that?' he asked. 'Please, don't start philosophizing! Vodka's for drinking, sturgeon's for eating, women for visiting and snow for walking over. Please try and behave like a normal human being, at least for one evening!'

'Don't worry, I'm not chickening out!' Vasilyev laughed.

The vodka warmed his chest. He looked at his friends affectionately, and admired and envied them. How well-balanced these healthy, strong, cheerful men were, how well-rounded and smooth their minds and hearts! They sang, loved the theatre passionately, sketched, talked a great deal, drank without having hangovers the next day. They were romantic, dissolute, gentle and audacious. They could work, be deeply indignant, laugh at nothing and talk rubbish. They were warm, decent, selfless and as human beings were in no way inferior to Vasilyev himself, who was so careful with his every word and step, so mistrustful, so cautious, so prone to make an issue out of the least trifle. And so he had felt the urge to spend just one evening in the same way as his friends, to unwind, let himself go a little. Would he have to drink vodka? Then drink it he would, even if he had a splitting headache the next morning. Would they take him to visit some girls? Then he would go. He would laugh, play the fool, cheerfully respond to passers-by.

He was laughing as he left the restaurant. He liked his friends – the one with pretensions to artistic eccentricity in that crumpled, broad-brimmed hat, the other in his sealskin cap – he had money, but he liked to play the academic Bohemian.

He liked the snow, the pale street-lamps, the sharp black prints left on the snow by the feet of passers-by. He liked the air and particularly that crystal-clear, gentle, innocent, almost virginal mood that one sees in nature only twice a year – when all is covered with snow, and on bright days or those moonlit nights in spring, when the ice breaks up on the river.

> 'Unwilling to these sad shores
> A mysterious force is drawing me . . .'

he sang under his breath.

For some reason he and his friends could not get that

tune out of their minds and the three of them sang it mechanically, out of time with each other.

Vasilyev pictured himself and his friends knocking at some door in ten minutes' time, creeping down dark passages, through dark rooms, to the women. Taking advantage of the darkness he would strike a match and suddenly illumine a suffering face and guilty smile. The woman – a mysterious blonde or brunette – would doubtless have her hair hanging down and be wearing a white nightdress. She would be frightened by the light and be terribly embarrassed. 'For goodness' sake, what are you doing?' she would ask. 'Put that light out.' It was all very terrifying, yet intriguing and novel.

II

The friends turned off Trubny Square into Grachovka Street and quickly went down the side-street which Vasilyev knew only by hearsay. Seeing two rows of houses with brightly lit windows and wide-open doors, hearing the gay sounds of pianos and fiddles floating out of all the doorways and mingling to create some weird musical jumble as if an invisible orchestra was tuning up in the darkness above the roofs, he was amazed and said, 'So many houses!'

'That's nothing!' the medical student said. 'There's ten

times as many in London – there's about a hundred thousand women like these living there.'

The cab drivers sat on their boxes as calmly and apathetically as in any other street. And, as in any other street, pedestrians walked the pavements. No one hurried, no one hid his face in his coat-collar, no one shook his head reproachfully ... In this indifference, this cacophony of pianos and fiddles, in those bright windows and wide-open doors, there was something quite blatant, brazen, bold and happy-go-lucky. In slave markets long ago it must have been just as busy and bustling, people's faces and walk must have shown the same indifference.

'Let's begin at the beginning,' the art student said.

The friends entered a narrow passage lit by a lamp with a reflector. When they opened the door a man in a black frock-coat, with the unshaven face and sleepy eyes of a flunkey, lazily got up from a yellow sofa. The place smelt like a laundry with a splash of vinegar. A door led from the hall into a brightly lit room. The medical student and the artist stopped in this doorway, craned their necks and looked into the room together.

'Buona sera, signori!' the artist began, making a theatrical bow. 'Rigoletto, Huguenotti, Traviata!'

'Havana, Cucaracha, Pistoletto!' the medical student said, pressing his cap to his chest and bowing low.

Vasilyev stood behind them. He too wanted to perform

a theatrical bow, to say something ridiculous, but he could only smile, and the embarrassment he felt was almost a feeling of shame. Impatiently, he waited to see what would happen next. A small, fair girl of about seventeen or eighteen appeared in the doorway. Her hair was closely cropped and she wore a short blue frock with a white metallic pendant on her breast.

'Why are you standing in the doorway?' she asked. 'Take your coats off and come into the lounge.'

The medical and art students still talked mock-Italian as they entered the lounge. Hesitantly, Vasilyev followed them.

'Gentlemen, please take your coats off,' a servant said sternly. 'We can't have this.'

Besides the blonde, there was another girl in the lounge – very tall and plump, with a foreign-looking face and bare arms. She was sitting by the piano with patience cards spread out on her lap. She completely ignored the visitors.

'Where's the other young ladies?' the medical student asked.

'Having tea,' the blonde said. 'Stepan,' she called, 'go and tell the girls some students have come.'

A little later a third girl came into the lounge. She wore a bright red dress with blue stripes. Her face was heavily and clumsily made up, her forehead was hidden beneath her hair and her unblinking eyes had a frightened look.

After she came in she immediately started singing some song in a strong, coarse contralto. A fourth girl appeared, then a fifth . . .

Vasilyev found nothing novel or interesting in any of this. He felt as if it was not the first time he had seen a lounge, piano, mirror with cheap gilt frame, pendant, blue striped dress and empty indifferent faces like these. There was no trace of the darkness, the quiet, the secrecy, the guilty smile and all that he had been expecting and fearing.

It was all so ordinary, prosaic and uninteresting. Only one thing aroused his curiosity a little – this was the strange, seemingly deliberate bad taste evident in the cornices, the ludicrous paintings, dresses, pendant. There was something special, unusual, about this lack of taste.

'How cheap and stupid it all is!' thought Vasilyev. 'What is there in all this rubbish I can see now that might tempt any normal man, that would make him commit the dreadful sin of buying a human being for a rouble? Sinning for the sake of magnificence, beauty, grace, passion, good taste – that I can understand. But this is something different. What's worth sinning for in this place? But I mustn't think about it.'

'You there with the beard, get me some porter!' the blonde said to him. Vasilyev was suddenly embarrassed.

'With pleasure,' he said, politely bowing. 'Only you must forgive me, madam, I . . . hm . . . won't join you. I don't drink.'

Five minutes later the friends were heading for another brothel.

'Now then, why did you get her porter?' the medical student asked angrily. 'Think you're a millionaire! That's six roubles down the drain!'

'Why not let her have the pleasure if that's what she wanted?' Vasilyev said, defending himself.

'It was *Madam's* pleasure, not hers. They tell the girls to ask customers to treat them to drinks, and they're the ones who make the profit.'

'See the windmill,' the art student sang, 'now in ruins.'

After arriving at another brothel the friends stayed out in the hall without going into the lounge. As in the first house, a frock-coated figure with a flunkey's sleepy face rose from a sofa in the hall. As he looked at this servant, his face and shabby frock-coat, Vasilyev thought, 'What sufferings an ordinary simple Russian must have gone through before landing up here as a footman! Where was he before and what did he do? What lay in store for him? Was he married? Where was his mother, and did she know he was a servant in this place?' And now Vasilyev could not help paying attention first and foremost to the male servant in each house he called at. In one house – he reckoned it was the fourth – there was a frail, shrivelled-looking little flunkey with a watch-chain on his waist-coat. He was reading *The Leaflet* and paid no attention to the new arrivals. As he looked at his face Vasilyev concluded, for some reason, that a person with a face like his was capable of robbery, murder and perjury. And it really was a fascinating face, with its large forehead, grey eyes, squashed little nose, thin, tight lips and an expression that was at once stupid and insolent – like that of a young beagle in pursuit of a hare. Vasilyev thought that it would be nice to touch that man's hair to see if it was wiry or soft. It was probably wiry, like a dog's.

III

After two glasses of porter the art student suddenly became drunk and unnaturally lively.

'Let's go to another!' he commanded, waving his arms. 'I'll take you to the best!'

After taking his friends to what was, in his opinion, the best brothel, he expressed an urgent desire to dance a quadrille. The medical student started grumbling about having to pay the musicians a rouble, but agreed to join him. They started dancing.

The best house was just as dreadful as the worst. Here there were exactly the same mirrors, pictures, exactly the same hair-styles and dresses. Examining the furniture and costumes, Vasilyev understood that this was not exactly bad taste, but something that could be called the taste (and the style even) of S—Street. This style was to be found nowhere else, and there was something honest about its very ugliness, which had not come about by chance, but was the result of a long process of development. After visiting eight brothels, he was no longer startled by the colours of the dresses, the long trains, the garish ribbons, the sailor suits and the thick, violet make-up on the girls' cheeks. He saw that all this was correct and that if only one of these women had been dressed like a normal human being, or if one decent engraving had hung on the walls, then the entire tone of the whole street would have suffered.

'How clumsily they sell themselves!' he thought. 'Can't they understand that vice is tempting only when it's attractive and concealed – when it's wrapped up as virtue? Modest black dresses, pale faces, sad smiles and even darkness would have more of an effect than all this crude tinsel. The stupid girls! If they can't see that for themselves, then their customers should have taught them, shouldn't they?'

A young lady in Polish costume, with white fur trimming, came over and sat by him. 'You're a nice dark and handsome man, why aren't you dancing?' she asked. 'Why do you look so bored?'

'Because I *am* bored.'

'Treat me to some claret, then you won't be bored.'

Vasilyev didn't reply. After a short pause he asked, 'What time do you go to bed?'

'After five.'

'And when do you get up?'

'Sometimes at two, sometimes three.'

11

'And what do you do when you're up?'

'We drink coffee and have dinner between six and seven.'

'And what do you eat?'

'Nothing special. Soup or cabbage stew, steak, dessert. Madam looks after her girls well. But why are you asking all this?'

'Hm, well, just to make conversation.'

Vasilyev wanted to discuss many things with the girl. He felt a strong urge to know where she was born; whether her parents were still alive; if they knew she was in this place; how had she come here; whether she was cheerful and contented, or if she was sad and oppressed by dismal thoughts; if she had hopes of escaping from her present situation one day. But try as he might, he just did not know where to start and how to frame his questions without appearing indiscreet. After a long, thoughtful silence he asked, 'How old are you?'

'Eighty,' the girl said, joking and laughing at the way the art student was comically waving his arms and legs about.

Suddenly she burst out laughing at something and produced a long, obscene sentence that everyone could hear. Vasilyev was struck dumb and, not knowing what kind of face to make, forced himself to smile. But only he was smiling, all the others – his friends, the musicians and the women – didn't even look at the girl sitting next to him. It was just as if they hadn't heard.

'Bring me some claret!' the girl repeated.

Vasilyev felt disgusted by those white trimmings and the girl's voice and he left her. He felt hot, that he was suffocating, and his heart started beating slowly, with strong hammer-like beats.

'Let's get out of here!' he said, tugging the art student's sleeve.

'Wait a minute, let me finish.'

While the art student and medical student were finishing their quadrille, Vasilyev scrutinized the musicians to avoid looking at the women. At the piano was a fine-looking old man in spectacles who resembled Marshal Bazaine. The violinist was a young man dressed in the latest fashion, and he had a fair, diminutive beard. His face was far from stupid, didn't look haggard – on the contrary, it was young, clever and fresh. He was fastidiously, tastefully dressed and he played with feeling. There was one problem: how did he and that respectable, handsome old man come to be here? Why weren't they ashamed to be playing in such a place? What did they think when they looked at the women?

If the pianist and violinist had been scruffy, hungry, miserable, drunken, with gaunt or stupid faces, their presence would perhaps have been understandable. But as things were, Vasilyev understood nothing. He remembered the story of the fallen woman that he had once read, but he found that image of humanity with the guilty smile had nothing in common with what he was seeing now. He felt that he wasn't watching prostitutes, but some kind of different, decidedly peculiar, alien and incomprehensible world. Had he seen that world before in the theatre, or read about it in a book, he would never have believed in it . . .

The woman with the white fur trimmings produced another loud laugh and called out something quite revolting. Overcome with disgust, Vasilyev blushed and left.

'Wait a moment, we're coming too!' the art student shouted after him.

IV

'I had a little chat with my partner while we were dancing,' the medical student told them when all three were out in the street. 'It was about her first love affair. The hero was some book-keeper from Smolensk, with a wife and five children. She was seventeen and lived with her mother and father who sold soap and candles.'

'How did he win her heart?' Vasilyev asked.

'He bought her fifty roubles' worth of underwear. The devil only knows what!'

'All the same, the medical student made his partner tell him all about her affair,' Vasilyev thought. 'But I didn't manage to . . .'

'Gentlemen, I'm going home,' he said.

'Why?'

'Because I don't know how to behave in a place like this. Besides, I feel bored and disgusted. It doesn't exactly cheer you up, does it? If only they were human, but they're savages, animals. I'm off, do what you like!'

'Oh, come on, dear Grigory, Grig . . .' the art student said, trying to coax him and putting his arm around him. 'Let's visit just one more, then to hell with them. Please, Gregorius!'

They persuaded Vasilyev and led him up some staircase. The carpet, gilt banisters, the porter who opened the door, the panelling in the hall were all in S— Street style, but elegant and imposing.

'Really, I ought to go home,' Vasilyev said, taking off his coat.

'Come on, old man,' the art student said, kissing his neck. 'Don't be childish, Grig-Grig, be a sport! Together we came, together we shall leave. You really are an ass, you know.'

'I can wait in the street. Christ, it's really disgusting here!'

'Now, now, Grigory. If it disgusts you, then you can make some observations. Do you understand? Make observations!'

'One should look at things objectively,' the medical student said pompously.

Vasilyev went into the lounge and sat down. Besides him and his friends there were several other visitors:

15

two infantry officers, a balding, grey-haired man in gold-rimmed spectacles, two beardless young men from the Institute of Surveyors and one very drunken man with the face of an actor. The girls were all busy with them and paid no attention to Vasilyev. Only one of them, dressed as Aida, gave him a sidelong glance, smiled for some reason and said with a yawn, 'Someone with dark hair has arrived.'

Vasilyev's heart pounded and his face burned. He was ashamed to face the other visitors, and it was a nasty, painful feeling. It was sheer agony to think that a respectable, loving person like himself (he had always looked upon himself as such) hated those women and felt only revulsion for them. He felt no pity for the women, nor the musicians, nor the servants.

'It's because I'm not trying to understand them,' he thought. 'They're more like animals than human beings – all of them – but they are human beings nonetheless, they have souls. One must understand them first and then judge them.'

'Grigory, don't go, wait for us!' the art student shouted and disappeared. The medical student soon disappeared too.

'Yes, I must try and understand them, this is no good,' Vasilyev kept thinking.

He began staring intensely into each woman's face, looking for a guilty smile. Either he was no good at reading expressions or not one of the women in fact felt guilty, but all he discovered on each face was a blank look of banal, workaday boredom and contentment. Stupid eyes, stupid smiles, harsh, stupid voices, provocative movements – that was all. In the past every one of them had clearly had an affair with a book-keeper and had fifty roubles' worth of underclothes, and now their only pleasures in life were the coffee, three-course dinners, wine, quadrilles and sleeping until two in the afternoon.

Not finding one guilty smile, Vasilyev looked for an intelligent face. His attention was caught by one that was pale, rather sleepy and tired: this was a brunette, no longer young, with a dress covered in sequins. She was sitting in an armchair looking thoughtfully at the floor. Vasilyev paced up and down and then sat by her, as if by accident.

'I must begin with something trite,' he thought, 'and then gradually move on to serious matters.'

'That's a pretty dress you're wearing!' he said and touched the gilt fringe of her shawl.

'Am I?' the brunette said lifelessly.

'Where are you from?'

'Me? A long way away, from Chernigov.'

'It's nice there, very pleasant.'

'The grass grows greener . . .'

'A pity I'm no good at describing nature,' Vasilyev thought. 'I could move her with descriptions of the Chernigov countryside. She must have loved it if that's where she was born.'

'Don't you find it boring here at times?' he asked.

'Of course.'

'Then why don't you leave if you're bored?'

'Where could I go? Begging for charity?'

'Begging would be easier than living here.'

'How do you know? Have you ever tried it?'

'Yes, I have, when I couldn't pay my tuition fees. Even if I hadn't, the thing should be obvious. Whatever you may say, a beggar is a free person, but you're a slave.'

The brunette stretched and sleepily watched a waiter carrying glasses and soda-water on a tray.

'Get me some porter,' she said, yawning again.

'Porter?' thought Vasilyev. 'But what if your brother or mother were to come in right now? What would you say? What would they say? They'd give you porter all right!'

Suddenly there was a sound of crying. Out of the adjoining room where the waiter had taken the soda-water rushed a fair-haired man with red face and angry eyes, followed by the tall, plump Madam.

'No one gave you permission to slap girls' faces,' she screeched. 'We have better-class clients than you and they don't start fights! You lousy fraud!'

A great racket ensued, startling Vasilyev and making him turn pale. In the next room someone was sobbing the deeply felt sobs of the cruelly abused. And he understood that here were real human beings who were being badly treated, who suffered, wept and cried out for help like people anywhere else. Intense loathing and disgust gave way to a feeling of acute pity and of anger with the offender. He rushed to the room where the sobs were coming from and between rows of bottles on a marble table top he could make out a martyred, tear-stained face. He stretched his hands towards this face, took one step towards the table, but immediately recoiled in horror. The weeping girl was drunk.

As he forced his way through the noisy crowd that had gathered around the fair-haired man, his heart sank, he felt the terror of a child, imagining that the inhabitants of this alien, incomprehensible world wanted to chase him, beat him and shower him with obscenities. He grabbed his coat from the hook and dashed headlong downstairs.

V

Pressing himself to the fence, Vasilyev stood near the house and waited for his friends to come out. The cheerful, bold, impudent and melancholy sounds of pianos and fiddles blended into a musical jumble which again resembled an invisible orchestra tuning up in the darkness over the roofs. If one looked up at this darkness the entire black background was sprinkled with moving white dots – falling snow. When the flakes came into the light they circled lazily in the air, like down, and fell even more lazily to earth. A mass of them swirled around

Vasilyev and clung to his beard, eyelashes, eyebrows. Cabmen, horses and passers-by were white all over.

'How can snow fall in *this* street!' Vasilyev wondered. 'Damn these brothels!'

His legs were giving way from the effort of running downstairs, he gasped as though he were climbing a hill, he heard his heart pounding, and he had an overwhelming desire to escape from that street as quickly as he could and go home. But he felt an even stronger desire to wait for his friends and vent his spleen on them. There was a great deal that he did not understand about these houses, and the minds of those doomed women were just as much of an enigma as before. But things were far worse than he ever could have imagined – that was clear. If the guilty woman in the story could be called 'fallen' then it was difficult to find a suitable name for all those who were dancing now to that jumble of sounds, who were producing those long, obscene sentences. They were not merely doomed, they were ruined.

'There is vice here,' he thought, 'but no awareness of guilt or hope of salvation. Those women are bought and sold, they are swamped with wine and all kinds of loathsome things, but they are just like sheep – unquestioning, complacent. Oh, good God!'

He could also see that all that went under the name of human dignity, individuality, the image and semblance of God, was defiled – 'down to the last drop' as drunks put it, and that not only were the street and stupid women to be blamed for this.

A crowd of students passed by, white with snow and cheerfully talking and laughing. One of them, tall and thin, stopped, peered into Vasilyev's face and said in a drunken voice, 'He's from our year! Sloshed are you, old chap? Aha! Never mind, enjoy yourself! Let yourself go! Don't be down in the dumps, old man!'

He took Vasilyev by the shoulders, pressed his cold wet moustache to his cheek, then slipped and staggered. Throwing up both arms he shouted, 'Hold on, mind you don't fall!'

In fits of laughter he ran off to catch up with his friends.

Through all the noise the art student's voice could be heard: 'How dare you strike a woman! I won't stand for it, blast you! You rotten swine!'

The medical student appeared in the doorway. He looked to both sides and when he saw Vasilyev he said anxiously, 'So here you are. Listen to me, you can't take Yegor anywhere! I don't understand him. He's made a real scene! Yegor, can you hear?' he shouted into the doorway. 'Yegor!'

The art student's shrill voice rang out from above: 'I won't allow you to strike a woman!'

Something heavy and cumbersome rolled down the stairs. It was the art student, flying head over heels: evidently he was being thrown out.

He struggled to his feet, shook his hat and brandished his fist upwards with a spiteful, outraged look.

'Bastards!' he shouted. 'Crooks! Bloodsuckers! I won't allow beating! Striking a defenceless, drunken woman! Oh, you . . .'

'Yegor! Come on, Yegor!' the medical student pleaded. 'I give you my word of honour that I'll never go out with you again. Word of honour!'

The art student gradually calmed down and the friends went home.

> 'Unwilling to these sad shores
> A mysterious force is drawing me . . .'

sang the medical student.

> 'See the windmill now in ruins'

the art student joined in a little later. 'God, how it's snowing! Grigory, why did you leave? You're a coward, an old woman, that's what!'

Vasilyev walked behind his friends and looked at their backs. 'It's one thing or another,' he thought. 'Either we only imagine prostitution's an evil and we exaggerate it. Or else, if it is in fact such a great evil as is commonly thought, then my dear friends are slave-owners, rapists and murderers just as much as those inhabitants of Syria and Cairo whose pictures one sees in *Niva*.* Now they're

---

* *Niva* (*The Cornfield*): a weekly illustrated magazine.

singing away, roaring with laughter, soberly arguing, but haven't *they* just been exploiting hunger, ignorance and stupidity? What they did . . . well, I saw it. What became of their humanity, their medicine, their painting? The learning, fine arts and elevated feelings of those murderers reminds me of the story of the bacon. Two robbers cut a beggar's throat in a forest. They start sharing out his clothes and find a piece of bacon in his bag. "That's good," one of them says. "Let's eat it." "Have you gone crazy?" the other asks, horrified. "Have you forgotten today's Wednesday, a fast day?" So they left it. Two men cut someone's throat and then emerge from the forest convinced they are devout Christians! Those two are the same; they buy women and go around thinking what fine artists and scholars they are . . .'

'Now listen!' he snapped. 'Why do you come here? Can't you see what horrors lie here? Medicine tells you that every single one of these women dies prematurely from tuberculosis or some other illness. The arts tell us that, morally, she's dead long before that. Let's suppose one of these women dies from entertaining an average of five hundred men in her life. Each of them is killed by five hundred men. Now, if you were each to visit this or similar places two hundred and fifty times during your lives, then the two of you would be responsible for the murder of one woman. Do you understand? Isn't it terrible? Two, three, five of you ganging together to kill one stupid, hungry woman! God, doesn't that horrify you?'

'I knew it would come to this,' the art student said, frowning. 'We should never have got mixed up with this imbecile. You think your head's full of great thoughts and ideas, don't you? Damned if I know what they are, but they're not ideas! You look at me now with loathing and disgust, but in my opinion you'd do better busying yourself building another twenty brothels like these than going around with a face like that. There's more depravity in that look of yours than in the whole street! Let's go, Volodya, to hell with him! He's nothing more than a moron, a complete imbecile . . .'

'We human beings do kill each other,' the medical student said. 'Of course that's immoral, but all these theories won't help. Goodbye!'

On Trubny Square the friends said goodbye and went their ways. Left to himself, Vasilyev strode down the boulevard. He was frightened of the dark, of the snow that was falling in large flakes, wanting to blanket the whole world, it seemed. He was afraid of the lamplight dimly glimmering through the snow clouds. An inexplicable, cowardly fear gripped him. Now and again he met passers-by, but he timidly kept out of their way, under the illusion that women, only women, were coming towards him from all directions and staring at him from all sides. 'It's starting,' he thought. 'I'm having a nervous breakdown.'

V I

At home he lay on his bed, shaking all over. 'They're alive, alive!' he said. 'God, they're alive!'

He indulged in every kind of fantasy, imagining himself first as a prostitute's brother, then as her father, then as the woman herself with her thickly powdered cheeks, and all of it horrified him.

For some reason he felt that he just had to solve the problem there and then, and at all costs. He felt that it was *his* problem and no one else's. He strained every nerve, overcame the despair inside him and sat on the bed, head clasped, trying to think how he could save all the women he had seen that day. Being an educated man, he was very familiar with the correct procedure for solving all kinds of problems. And for all his agitation he strictly adhered to that routine. He recalled the history of the problem, its literature, and between three and four o'clock in the morning he paced his room trying to remember all the modern methods of saving women. He had many good friends and acquaintances living in rooms at Falzstein's, Galyashkin's, Nechayev's, Yechkin's. Among them were quite a number of honest, selfless men. Some of them had tried to save women.

'These few attempts,' thought Vasilyev, 'can be divided into three groups. Some have ransomed a woman from a brothel, rented a room for her, bought her a sewing-machine and she has become a seamstress. Whether he wanted to or not, her rescuer has made her his mistress and then departed the scene after graduating, handing her over to another decent chap as though she were some object. And the woman has remained fallen. Others, having redeemed a woman and also rented a separate room for her, have bought the obligatory sewing-machine and started her on reading and writing, given her moral tuition and supplied books. As long as this was interesting and novel for the woman, she has stayed with the man and got on with her sewing. But later, growing bored, she has started entertaining men behind the moral tutor's back. Or else she has run back to the place where she could sleep until three in the afternoon, drink coffee and eat as much as she liked. A third group, the most zealous and selfless of all, have taken a bold, decisive step. They have married the girl. And when that shameless, downtrodden, spoilt or stupid animal has become a wife, mistress of the house and then a mother, this has so transformed her life and outlook that it has become hard to recognize a former prostitute in this wife and mother. Yes, marriage is the best and perhaps the only way.'

'But that's impossible!' Vasilyev said out loud and slumped on to the bed. 'I'm the last kind of person to marry! One has to be a saint for that, incapable of hatred or revulsion. But let's suppose that the medical student, the art student and myself overcame our apprehension and married. Supposing they all married? What would be the outcome? The outcome would be, while they were getting married here, in Moscow, the Smolensk book-keeper would be corrupting a new batch of them, and this other batch would come pouring into this place to fill the vacancies, together with girls from Saratov, Nizhny-Novgorod, Warsaw . . . And what about those hundred thousand prostitutes from London? And from Hamburg?'

The oil in his lamp had burnt down and it had begun to smoke. Vasilyev did not notice. Once again he paced backwards and forwards, still deep in thought. Now he framed the question differently: how could one remove the need for prostitutes? To achieve this, the men who bought and murdered these women should be made to realize the whole immorality of their role as slave-owners and be duly horrified. It was the men who had to be saved.

'Science and the arts won't be any help here,' Vasilyev thought. 'The only way is by "spreading the word".'

And he began to imagine himself standing next evening on a street corner, asking every passer-by, 'Where are you going and why? Why don't you fear God?'

He would address apathetic cabmen: 'Why are you hanging about here? Why don't you protest, show your indignation? Surely you believe in God and know that it's a sin for which people go to hell? So why can't you speak up? I know they're strangers to you, but please understand that they have fathers, brothers just like you . . . yes!'

Once, a friend of Vasilyev's had said that he was a gifted man. People are usually gifted in literature, drama, the fine arts, but his special gift was for human beings. He was keenly, marvellously sensitive to all forms of pain. Just as a good actor reflects the movements and voices of others, so Vasilyev could reflect another's pain in his soul. He would weep at the sight of tears. Among the sick, he himself became ill and would groan. If he saw an act of violence he would feel that he was the victim, would behave cowardly, like a child, and run off panic-stricken. Other people's pain irritated and stimulated him, reduced him to ecstasy, and so on.

I don't know whether this friend was right, but when Vasilyev thought that he had solved his problem his mood became inspired. He wept, laughed, spoke out loud the words he was going to say the next day and felt an intense love for those who would accept his teaching and join him on the street corner to spread the word. He sat down to write letters and made vows . . .

All this was like inspiration in that it was short-lived – Vasilyev soon became tired. The very weight of numbers of those prostitutes from London, Hamburg, Warsaw pressed down on him as mountains press down on the earth, and made him quail and panic. He remembered that he had no gift for words, that he was cowardly and faint-hearted, that apathetic people would hardly want to listen to him, a timid, insignificant third-year law student, and that true evangelism involves actions as well as sermons.

When it was light and carriages were already clattering down the street, Vasilyev lay motionless on his couch, vacantly staring. No longer was he thinking about women, or men, or spreading the word. His entire attention was riveted on the mental anguish that was tormenting him. It was a dull, abstract, vague kind of pain, rather like a feeling of hopelessness, despair and the most terrible fear. He could point it out – it was in his chest, below the heart. But he knew of nothing with which he could compare it. In his life he had suffered severe toothache, pleurisy and neuralgia, but all that was nothing compared with this spiritual pain. With that kind of pain, life was repellent. The dissertation, the fine work he had written, the people he loved, the rescue of fallen women, together with the memory of all that he had loved or had been indifferent to only yesterday, irritated him now as much as the clatter of carriages, the scurrying of servants, the daylight. If someone were to perform some great deed of mercy or dreadful act of violence before him at that moment, both would have equally revolted him. Of all the thoughts lazily drifting through his mind only two did not irritate him: one was that he had the power to kill himself at any moment and the other – that the pain would not last more than three days. The latter he knew from experience.

After lying down for a while he stood up, wrung his hands and stopped pacing the room from corner to corner, moving in a square, along the walls, instead. He looked at himself in the mirror. His face was pale and hollow-cheeked, his temples were sunken, his eyes had become bigger, darker and less mobile, as if they belonged to a stranger, and they expressed unbearable mental suffering.

At noon the art student knocked at the door.

'Grigory, are you in?' he asked.

Not receiving any reply he stood there for a moment, pondered and then answered himself in Ukrainian dialect,

'Ain't no one thar. 'E's darned well gone off to that looniversity, blast 'im!'

And he went away. Vasilyev lay down on his bed, covered his head with the pillow and started crying out with pain. The more abundantly the tears flowed the worse his mental anguish became. When it grew dark he thought of the night of torment that awaited him and he was overwhelmed by the most dreadful despair. Quickly, he dressed, ran from his room, leaving the door wide open and, without aim or reason, went out into the street. Without asking himself where he was going he swiftly went down Sadovy Street.

It was snowing as heavily as yesterday, but the snow was thawing. With his hands in his sleeves, shivering and starting at the clatter, the bells of horse-trams, and passers-by, Vasilyev walked down Sadovy Street as far as the Sukharev Tower, then to the Red Gate, where he turned off into Basmanny Street. He went into a tavern and drank a large vodka, but this did not make him feel any better. After reaching Razgulyay, he turned right and strode down side-streets where he had never been before. He reached the old bridge where the River Yauza roars past and from where one can see the long rows of lights in the windows of the Red Barracks. To relieve his mental torment with some new sensation or other kind of pain, and not knowing the best way to go about this, Vasilyev unbuttoned his overcoat and frock-coat, weeping and trembling, and bared his chest to the sleet and wind. But that brought no relief either. Then he bent over the railing on the bridge, looked down at the black, turbulent Yauza and felt a strong urge to throw himself in, head first – not from disgust with life, not to commit suicide, but to replace one pain with another, even if it meant being broken to pieces. But the black water, the darkness, the desolate snowy banks terrified him. He shuddered and moved on. After passing the Red Barracks he returned, went down into a small wood and then came out on to the bridge again.

'No, I'm going home! Home!' he thought. 'It will be better there.' And home he went. Once there he tore his wet overcoat and cap off and started pacing along the walls, never tiring. He kept this up until morning.

VII

When the artist and the medical student called next morning, he was dashing around the room groaning with pain. His shirt was torn and his hands bitten.

'For God's sake!' he sobbed when he saw his friends. 'Take me where you like, do what you want, but hurry up, save me, for God's sake! I shall kill myself!'

The art student was very taken aback and turned pale. The medical student too was close to tears, but remembering that doctors had to keep calm and collected in all eventualities, said coldly, 'You're having a nervous breakdown. But don't worry, we'll go to a doctor's right away.'

'Wherever you like, only quickly, for God's sake!'

'Now don't get excited. You must take a grip on yourself.'

With trembling hands the art student and medical student dressed Vasilyev and led him out into the street. On the way the medical student told him, 'Mikhail Sergeyevich has been wanting to meet you for ages. He's very nice and knows his stuff. Although he only graduated in 1882 he has a huge practice already. He's very matey with students.'

'Get a move on, hurry!' Vasilyev said.

Mikhail Sergeyevich, a stout, fair-haired doctor, greeted the friends solemnly, with an icy civility, and he smiled on only one side of his face.

'Mayer and the art student have told me about your illness,' he said. 'Very glad to be of service. Well, now, please sit down.'

He made Vasilyev sit in a large armchair near the table and moved a box of cigarettes over to him.

'Well, now,' he began, smoothing the knees of his trousers. 'Let's get down to business. How old are you?'

He began to ask questions, which the medical student answered. He asked if Vasilyev's father had ever suffered from any particular illness, if he was a hard drinker, if he was unusually cruel or had any other peculiarities. He asked precisely the same questions about his grandfather, mother, sisters and brothers. When he learned that his mother had an excellent voice and had sometimes been on the stage, he suddenly livened up and asked, 'Forgive me, but can you remember if the stage was an obsession with your mother?'

Twenty minutes passed. Vasilyev grew bored with the doctor smoothing his knees and harping on the same thing.

'As far as I can tell from your questions, Doctor,' he said, 'you want to know if my illness is hereditary or not. It is *not*.'

The doctor went on to ask if Vasilyev had had any secret vices at all in his childhood, whether there had been head injuries, strong enthusiasms, idiosyncrasies, obsessions. It's possible to avoid giving answers to half the questions

33

posed by diligent doctors without endangering one's health in the slightest, but Mikhail Sergeyevich, the medical student and the art student all wore expressions that seemed to say: if Vasilyev fails to answer just one question, then all is lost. For some reason the doctor wrote down the answers on a piece of paper. When he learned that Vasilyev had graduated from the Natural Sciences Faculty and was now a student in the Faculty of Law, the doctor became very pensive.

'Last year he wrote a first-class dissertation,' the medical student said.

'I'm sorry, but please don't interrupt. I can't concentrate,' the doctor said, smiling on one side of his face. 'Yes, of course, that has a part to play in the case history. Intense mental effort, over-tiredness . . . Yes, yes. And do you drink vodka?' he asked, turning to Vasilyev.

Another twenty minutes passed. In a low voice, the medical student began expounding his theory as to the immediate cause of the attack and then told him that he, the art student and Vasilyev had gone to S—Street the day before yesterday.

The indifferent, restrained, offhand tone in which his friends and the doctor spoke about women and that miserable side-street struck Vasilyev as most strange.

'Please tell me one thing, Doctor,' he said, trying not to appear rude. 'Is prostitution an evil or isn't it?'

'My dear fellow, who's disputing it?' the doctor said,

his expression seeming to say that he had long ago solved all these problems. 'Who's disputing it?'

'Are you a psychiatrist?' Vasilyev asked rudely.

'Yes, I'm a psychiatrist.'

'Perhaps you're all right!' Vasilyev said, rising to his feet and starting to pace the room. 'You could well be! But I find it really amazing! The fact that I've studied in two faculties is considered a great achievement. I'm praised to the skies for writing a dissertation that will be ignored and forgotten in three years' time. But because I can't discuss fallen women as nonchalantly as I might talk about these chairs, I'm given medical treatment, called insane and pitied!'

Vasilyev somehow felt dreadfully sorry for himself, his friends, for all those he had seen the day before yesterday, and for the doctor. He burst into tears and fell back into the armchair.

His friends gave the doctor an inquiring look. His expression suggesting that he considered himself a specialist in this field, the doctor went over to Vasilyev and, without speaking to him, gave him some drops to drink. Then, when he had calmed down, he made him undress and started testing the sensitivity of his skin, his knee reflexes, and so on.

Vasilyev felt better. When he left the doctor's he felt ashamed of himself. The clatter of carriages no longer irritated him and the heavy weight beneath his heart grew lighter and lighter, just as if it were melting away. He held two prescriptions: one for potassium bromide, the other for morphia. He had taken all that kind of thing before!

He stood in the street and pondered for a moment. Saying goodbye to his friends he lazily trudged along to the university.

The Black Monk

I

Andrey Vasilich Kovrin, MA, was exhausted, his nerves were shattered. He did not take any medical treatment but mentioned his condition in passing to a doctor friend over a bottle of wine, and was advised to spend the spring and summer in the country. And as it happened he received just then a long letter from Tanya Pesotskaya, inviting him to come and stay at Borisovka. So he decided he really must get away.

At first – this was in April – he went to his own estate, Kovrinka, where he lived on his own for three weeks. Then after waiting until the roads were passable, he drove off in a carriage to see his former guardian and mentor Pesotsky the horticulturalist, who was famous throughout Russia. It was no more than about fifty miles from Kovrinka to Pesotsky's place at Borisovka and it was pure joy travelling along the soft road in spring, in a comfortable sprung carriage.

Pesotsky's house was huge, with columns, peeling plaster lions, and a footman in coat and tails at the entrance.

37

The gloomy, severe, old-fashioned park was strictly laid out in the landscaped English style, stretched almost half a mile from the house to the river, and ended in a precipitous clayey bank where pines grew, their exposed roots resembling shaggy paws. Down below, the water glinted uninvitingly, sandpipers flew past squeaking plaintively, and it was generally the kind of place to make you want to sit down and write a ballad. But near the house itself, in the courtyard and the orchard, which took up about eighty acres, including the nursery beds, it was cheerful and lively, even in bad weather. Nowhere, except at Pesotsky's, had Kovrin seen such wonderful roses, lilies, camellias, so many different tulips, with colours ranging from white to soot-black, such a profusion of flowers. It was only the beginning of spring and the real splendours of the flowerbeds were still hidden in the hothouses. But the flowers in bloom along the paths – and here and there in the beds – were enough to make you feel that you were in the very kingdom of tender hues as you strolled in the garden, especially early in the morning, when dew sparkled on every petal.

The ornamental section of the garden, which Pesotsky disparagingly called 'sheer nonsense', had seemed like a fairyland to Kovrin as a child. The oddities, elaborate monstrosities and travesties of nature that were to be seen here! There were trellised fruit trees, a pear tree shaped like a Lombardy poplar, globe-shaped oaks and limes, an apple tree umbrella, arches, initials, candelabra, and even an '1862' made from plums – this was the year Pesotsky first took up horticulture. Here also were fine, graceful saplings with straight, firm stems like palm trees, and only after a very close look could you tell that they were gooseberries or blackcurrants. But what most of all made the garden a cheerful, lively place was the constant activity. From dawn to dusk gardeners with wheelbarrows, hoes and watering-cans swarmed like ants near the trees and bushes, on the paths and flowerbeds.

Kovrin arrived at the Pesotskys' after nine in the evening. He found Tanya and her father Yegor Semyonych in a terribly worried state. The clear, starry sky and the thermometer foretold frost towards morning, but the head gardener Ivan Karlych had gone off to town and there was no one left they could rely on.

During supper, they talked only of this morning frost and decided that Tanya would not go to bed, but would go round the orchard after midnight to check if everything was all right, while Yegor Semyonych would get up at three, even earlier perhaps. Kovrin sat with Tanya the whole evening and after midnight went with her into the garden. It was cold and there was a strong smell of burning. In the big orchard, called 'commercial' as it brought Yegor Semyonych several thousand roubles profit every year, a dense, black, acrid smoke was spreading over the ground and enveloping the trees, saving all those thousands from the frost. Here the trees were planted like draughts pieces, in straight, even rows, like

39

columns of soldiers. This strict, pedantic regularity, plus the fact that all the trees were exactly the same height, all of them having absolutely identical crowns and trunks, made a monotonous, even boring picture. Kovrin and Tanya walked between the rows, where bonfires of manure, straw and all kind of refuse were smouldering, and every now and then they met workers drifting through the smoke like shadows. Only cherries, plums and certain varieties of apple were in bloom, but the whole orchard was drowning in smoke. Kovrin breathed a deep breath only when they reached the nurseries.

'When I was a child the smoke used to make me sneeze,' he said, shrugging his shoulders, 'but I still don't understand why this smoke saves the plants from frost.'

'Smoke is a substitute for clouds when the sky is clear . . .' Tanya said.

'But what use are *they*?'

'You don't normally get a frost when it's dull and overcast.'

'That's right!'

He laughed and took her arm. Her broad, very serious face, chill from the cold, with its fine black eyebrows, the raised coat collar which cramped her movements, her whole slim, graceful body, her dress tucked up from the dew – all this moved him deeply.

'Heavens, how you've grown up!' he said. 'Last time I left here, five years ago, you were still a child. You were so thin, long-legged, bareheaded, with that short little dress you used to wear. And I teased you and called you a heron . . . How time changes everything!'

'Yes, five years!' Tanya sighed. 'A lot of water has flowed under the bridge since then. Tell me, Andrey, in all honesty,' she said in an animated voice, peering into his face, 'have you grown tired of us? But why am I asking you this? You're a man, you live your own interesting life, you're an eminent person . . . Becoming like strangers to each other is really so natural! Anyway, Andrey, I want you to treat us as your family, we have a right to that.'

'But I do, Tanya.'

'Word of honour?'

'Yes, word of honour.'

'You were surprised before that we had so many of your photos. You must know Father idolizes you. At times I think he loves you more than me. He's proud of you. You are a scholar, a remarkable person, you've made a dazzling career for yourself and he's convinced this is because he brought you up. I let him think this, I don't see why I should stop him.'

Dawn was breaking – this was particularly evident from the clarity with which puffs of smoke and the tree tops were outlined now in the air. Nightingales were singing and the cries of quails came from the fields.

'But it's time for bed,' Tanya said. 'Besides that, it's cold.' She took his arm. 'Thanks for coming, Andrey. Our friends aren't very interesting, not that we have many.

41

nave is the garden, garden, garden, nothing else.'
laughed. 'First-class, second-class, Oporto, rennets
and winter apples, budding, grafting. Our whole life has
gone into this garden, I dream of nothing but apple and
pear trees. Of course, it's all very nice and useful, but
sometimes I want something else, to break the monotony.
I remember the times you came for the holidays, or just
for a short visit, how the house became somehow fresher
and brighter then, as though the covers had been taken
off the chandeliers and furniture. I was a little girl then,
but I did understand.'

She spoke for a long time and with great feeling. Suddenly Kovrin was struck by the idea that he might even
conceive an affection for this small, fragile, loquacious
creature during the course of the summer, become
attracted to her and fall in love. In their situation that
would be so natural and possible! He was both touched
and amused by the thought. He leant down towards that
dear, worried face and softly sang:

> Onegin, I will not hide it,
> I love Tatyana madly . . .

Yegor Semyonych was up already when they returned
to the house. Kovrin did not feel like sleeping, got into
conversation with the old man and went back to the
garden with him. Yegor Semyonych was a tall, broad-
shouldered man, with a large paunch. Although he
suffered from short breath, he always walked so fast it

was hard keeping up with him. He had an extremely worried look and was always hurrying off somewhere as if all would be lost should he be just one minute late.

'It's a peculiar thing, my dear boy,' he began, then paused for breath. 'As you see, it's freezing down on the ground, but just you hold a thermometer on a stick about twelve feet above it and you'll find it's warm there . . . Why is it?'

'I honestly don't know,' Kovrin said, laughing.

'Hm . . . one can't know everything of course . . . However capacious your brain is, it won't accommodate everything. Philosophy's more your line, isn't it?'

'I give lectures on psychology, but my main interest is philosophy.'

'And you're not bored?'

'On the contrary, it's my life.'

'Well, God bless you . . .' Yegor Semyonych murmured, thoughtfully stroking his grey side-whiskers. 'God bless you . . . I'm very pleased for you . . . very pleased, dear boy.'

But suddenly he pricked up his ears, pulled a horrified face, ran to one side and soon disappeared in the clouds of smoke behind the trees.

'Who tied a horse to that apple tree?' the despairing, heart-rending cry rang out. 'What swine, what scum dared to tie a horse to an apple tree? Good Lord! They've ruined, frozen, polluted, mucked everything up! The garden's ruined! Ruined! Oh, God!'

He went back to Kovrin, looking exhausted, outraged. 'What can you do with this confounded riff-raff?' he said tearfully, flinging his arms out helplessly. 'Last night Stepka was carting manure and tied his horse to the apple tree. He twisted the reins so hellishly tight, damn him, that the bark's rubbed off. How could he do it? I had words with him, but the idiot just stood gaping. Hanging's too good for him!'

After he had calmed down he put his arms round Kovrin and kissed him on the check. 'Well, God bless, God bless . . .' he muttered. 'I'm very pleased you came. I can't say how glad I am . . . Thanks.'

Then, at the same rapid pace and with that same worried look, he toured the whole garden, showing his former ward all the conservatories, greenhouses, cold frames, and the two apiaries he called the 'wonder of the century'.

As they walked along, the sun rose, filling the garden with a bright light. It grew warm. Anticipating a fine, cheerful, long day, Kovrin recalled that in fact it was only the beginning of May and that the whole summer lay ahead – just as bright, cheerful and long, and suddenly there welled up within him that feeling of radiant, joyous youth he had known in his childhood, when he had run around this garden. And he embraced the old man in turn and kissed him tenderly. Both of them, deeply moved, went into the house and drank tea from old-fashioned porcelain cups, with cream and rich pastries. These little things again reminded Kovrin of his childhood and youth. The beautiful present, the freshly awakened impressions of the past, blended together: they had a somewhat inhibiting effect, but none the less gave him a feeling of well-being.

He waited for Tanya to wake up, drank coffee with her, went for a stroll, and then returned to his room and sat down to work. He read attentively, took notes, now and again looking up at the open window or the fresh flowers that stood, still moist with dew, in vases on the table, then lowering his eyes on his book again; it seemed every vein in his body was pulsating and throbbing with pleasure.

II

In the country he continued to lead the same nervous, restless life as in town. He read and wrote a great deal, studied Italian, and on his strolls took pleasure in the thought that he would soon be back at work again. Everyone was amazed he slept so little. If he chanced to doze off during the day for half an hour, he could not sleep at all later and would emerge from a night of insomnia vigorous and cheerful, as if nothing was wrong.

He talked a lot, drank wine and smoked expensive cigars. Young ladies who lived nearby called on the Pesotskys almost every day and played the piano and sang with Tanya. Sometimes a young gentleman from the neighbourhood, an excellent violinist, would call. Kovrin would listen so hungrily to the playing and singing it tired him out, and the exhaustion was plainly visible from the way his eyelids seemed to stick together and his head dropped to one side.

One evening, after tea, he was sitting on the balcony reading. At the same time Tanya, who sang soprano, together with one of the young ladies – a contralto – and the young violinist, were practising Braga's famous *Serenade*. Kovrin listened hard to the words (they were Russian) but could not understand them at all. Finally, after putting his book aside and listening very closely, he did understand: a young girl, with a morbid imagination, was in her garden one night and heard some mysterious sounds, so beautiful and strange, she had to admit that their harmony was something divine, incomprehensible to mere mortals as it soared up again into the heavens whence it came. Kovrin began to feel sleepy. He rose to his feet, wearily walked up and down the drawing-room, then the ballroom. When the singing stopped, he took Tanya by the arm and went out onto the balcony with her.

'Since early this morning I haven't been able to get a certain legend out of my mind,' he said. 'I can't remember if I read it somewhere or if I heard it, but it's really quite strange – doesn't appear to make any sense at all. I should say from the start that it's not distinguished for its clarity. A thousand years ago a certain monk, dressed in black, was walking across a desert – somewhere in Syria or Arabia . . . A few miles from where he was walking a fisherman saw another black monk slowly moving across the surface of a lake. This second monk was a mirage. Now forget the laws of optics, which the legend apparently doesn't acknowledge, and listen to what happened next. The mirage produced another one. This second mirage produced a third, so that the image of the black monk began to be transmitted endlessly from one layer of the atmosphere to the other. He was sighted in Africa, then Spain, India, the far north . . . He finally left the earth's atmosphere and now wanders through the whole universe, never meeting the conditions which would make it possible for him to fade away. Perhaps he'll be seen somewhere on Mars now, or on some star in the Southern Cross. But, my dear, the essence, the real crux of the legend is this: precisely one thousand years after that monk first walked across the desert, the mirage will return to the earth's atmosphere and appear to people. And it seems these thousand years are almost up. According to the legend, we can expect the black monk any day now.'

'A strange mirage,' said Tanya, who did not care for the legend.

'But the most amazing thing is,' Kovrin said, laughing, 'I just can't remember what prompted me to think of it. Did I read it somewhere? Did I hear about it? Perhaps the black monk was only a dream? I swear to God, I can't remember. But I'm intrigued by this legend. I've been thinking about it all day.'

Leaving Tanya to her guests, he went out of the house and strolled by the flowerbeds, deep in thought. The sun was setting. The freshly watered flowers gave off a moist, irritating scent. In the house the singing had started again; from the distance the violin sounded like a human voice. Kovrin racked his brains trying to remember where he had read or heard about that legend as he walked unhurriedly towards the park, reaching the river before he knew where he was.

He descended the path that ran down a steep bank, past bare roots, to the water, where he disturbed some sandpipers and frightened two ducks away. Here and there on the gloomy pines gleamed the last rays of the setting sun, but evening had already come over the surface of the river. Kovrin crossed the footbridge to the other side. Before him lay a broad field full of young rye not yet in ear. There was no human habitation, not a living soul out there, and it seemed the path would lead him to that same unknown, mysterious spot where the sun had just set and where the evening glow spread its flames so magnificently over all that wide expanse.

'So much space, freedom, peace here!' Kovrin thought as he walked along the path. 'The whole world seems to be looking at me, has gone silent, and is waiting for me to understand it.'

But just then some ripples spread across the rye and a gentle evening breeze lightly caressed his bare head. A moment later there was another gust, stronger this time, and the rye rustled and he could hear the dull murmur of the pines behind him. Kovrin stood motionless in astonishment. On the horizon a tall black column was rising up into the sky, like a whirlwind or tornado. Its outlines were blurred, but he could see at once that it was not standing still, but moving at terrifying speed straight towards him – and the nearer it came, the smaller and clearer it grew. Kovrin leapt aside into the rye to make way – and he was only just in time . . . A monk in black vestments, grey-haired and with black eyebrows, his arms across his chest, flashed past; his bare feet did not touch the ground. After he had raced on another six yards he looked round at Kovrin, nodded and gave him a friendly, but artful, smile. What a pale, terribly pale, thin face though! Growing larger again, he flew across the river, struck the clayey bank and the pines without making a sound, passed straight through and disappeared into thin air.

'So, there it is . . .' murmured Kovrin. 'That shows there's truth in the legend.'

Without trying to find an explanation for this strange apparition and satisfied that he had managed to get such a close look, not only at the black vestments, but even at the monk's face and eyes, he went back to the house feeling pleasantly excited.

People were strolling peacefully in the park and

garden, the musicians were playing in the house, so only he had seen the monk. He had a strong urge to tell Tanya and Yegor Semyonych about everything, but he realized they would surely think the story crazy and be scared stiff. Better keep quiet about it. He laughed out loud, sang, danced a mazurka; he was in high spirits and everyone – Tanya, her guests – found that he really had a radiant, inspired look about him that evening, that he was most interesting.

III

After supper, when the guests had left, he went to his room and lay on the couch. He wanted to think about the monk, but a moment later in came Tanya.

'Here, Andrey, read Father's articles,' she said, handing him a bundle of pamphlets and offprints. 'They're wonderful, he's an excellent writer.'

'I wouldn't say that!' Yegor Semyonych said, forcing a laugh as he followed her into the room; he felt embarrassed. 'Don't listen to her, please! Don't read them! But if you need something to make you sleep, then go ahead. They're an excellent soporific!'

'In my opinion they're magnificent,' Tanya said with great conviction. 'Read them, Andrey, and persuade Father to write more often. He could write a whole course in horticulture.'

Yegor Semyonych gave a forced laugh, blushed and started speaking in the way shy authors usually do. In the end he gave in. 'In that case, read Gaucher's article first, then these short ones in Russian,' he muttered, turning over the pamphlets with trembling hands. 'Otherwise you won't understand a thing. Before you read my objections, you must know what it is I'm objecting to. However, it's rubbish . . . boring. What's more, I think it's time for bed.'

Tanya went out. Yegor Semyonych sat beside Kovrin on the couch and sighed deeply. 'Yes, my dear boy,' he began after a short silence. 'Yes, my dear Master of Arts. Here I am writing articles and exhibiting at shows and winning medals . . . They say Pesotsky has "apples as big as your head" and that he made his fortune with his orchard. Pesotsky is monarch of all he surveys, in short. But, you may ask, what's the point of it all? The garden is really beautiful, a show-garden in fact. It's not so much a garden as a complete institution, of the greatest importance to the state, a step, so to speak, towards a new era in Russian economics and industry. But what's the point of it? What's the use?'

'It speaks for itself.'

'That's not what I mean. I'd like to know, what will happen to the garden when I die? It won't be kept up to its present standard for more than one month. The secret of my success isn't that it's a big garden, with lots of gardeners, but because I love the work – do you follow?

Perhaps I love it better than myself. I work from dawn till dusk. The grafting, pruning, planting – I do them all myself. When people start helping me, I get jealous and irritated until I'm downright rude to them. The whole secret is *love*, and by that I mean the keen eye and head of the master looking after his own place, the feeling that comes over you when you've gone visiting for an hour and you just sit still. But your heart's not there, you're miles away – afraid something might be going wrong in the garden. And when I die who'll look after it? Who'll do the work? The head gardener? The ordinary gardeners? What do you think? So let me tell you, dear boy, the principal enemy in our work isn't hares, cockchafers or frost, but the man who doesn't care.'

'And Tanya?' laughed Kovrin. 'She couldn't possibly do more harm than a hare. She loves the work, she understands it.'

'Yes, she loves and understands it. If the garden passes into *her* hands after my death and she takes charge, I could hope for nothing better. But supposing she marries, God forbid?' Yegor Semyonych whispered and gave Kovrin a frightened look. 'This is my point! She'll marry, have children and then she'll have no time to think about the garden. But my main worry is her marrying some young whipper-snapper who'll grow greedy, rent the garden out to some market-woman and it'll all go to rack and ruin within a year! In this kind of business women are like the plague!'

Yegor Semyonych sighed and was silent for a few minutes. 'Perhaps it's just egotism, but I'm telling you quite frankly: I don't want Tanya to marry. I'm afraid! There's that young fop who comes here scraping his fiddle. I know Tanya won't marry him, I know that very well, but I just can't stand the sight of him. On the whole I'm quite a crank, dear boy. I admit it.' Yegor Semyonych got up and paced the room excitedly; it was plain he wanted to say something very important, but he couldn't bring himself to.

'I'm extremely fond of you and I'll be open with you,' he said at last, stuffing his hands into his pockets. 'I'm usually quite straight-forward when it comes to certain ticklish questions and I'm telling you exactly what I think – I can't stand these so-called "innermost thoughts". I'm telling you straight: you're the only man I wouldn't mind marrying my daughter. You're clever, you have feelings and you wouldn't let my beloved work perish. But the main reason is – I love you like a son . . . and I'm proud of you. If Tanya and yourself became fond of each other, well then, I'd be very glad, happy even. I'm telling you straight, without frills, as an honest man.'

Kovrin burst out laughing. Yegor Semyonych opened the door to go out and stopped on the threshold. 'If Tanya gave you a son I'd make a gardener out of him,' he said thoughtfully. 'However, that's an idle dream . . . Good night.'

Left alone, Kovrin settled himself more comfortably

on the couch and started on the articles. One bore the title *Intermedial Cultivation*, another *A few Observations on Mr Z's Remarks on Double-Trenching in New Gardens*, and another *More about Grafting Dormant Buds*; and there were other titles like that. But what a restless, uneven tone, what highly charged, almost pathological fervour! Here was an article with apparently the most inoffensive title and unexceptionable subject – the winter dessert apple. But Yegor Semyonych first weighed in with an *audiatur altera pars* and ended with *sapienti sat*, interpolating these dicta with a whole torrent of venomous animadversions apropos the 'learned ignorance of our self-appointed gentlemen-horticulturalists who look down on nature from their Olympian heights': or Gaucher, 'whose reputation was made by ignoramuses and dilettantes'. These remarks were followed by the totally irrelevant, forced, sham regret for the fact that it was no longer legal to birch peasants who stole fruit and damaged trees in the process.

'It's a fine, pleasant, healthy occupation, but even here it's passion and warfare,' Kovrin thought. 'Probably, it's because intellectuals are neurotic and over-sensitive everywhere, in all walks of life. Perhaps it can't be avoided.'

He thought of Tanya who liked Yegor Semyonych's articles so much. She was not tall, was pale and thin, with protruding collar-bones; her dark, clever, staring eyes were always peering, seeking something. She walked just like her father, taking short, quick steps. Very talkative, she loved to argue and would accompany the most trivial phrase with highly expressive mimicry and gesticulations. She was probably highly strung.

Kovrin read on, but he understood nothing and gave up. That same, agreeable feeling of excitement he had had when dancing his mazurka and listening to the music made him weary now and stirred a multitude of thoughts. He stood up and started walking round the room, thinking about the black monk. It occurred to him that if he alone had seen that strange, supernatural apparition, then he must be ill and a prey to hallucinations. This thought frightened him, but not for long.

'In fact I feel fine. I'm not harming anyone. So that means there's nothing bad in these hallucinations,' he thought and felt fine again.

He sat on the couch and clasped his head to hold in check that incomprehensible feeling of joy which filled his whole being; then he paced up and down again and started to work. But the ideas he found in the book left him unsatisfied. He wanted something gigantic, immense, staggering. Towards dawn he undressed and reluctantly got into bed. After all, he had to sleep!

When he heard Yegor Semyonych's footsteps receding into the garden, Kovrin rang the bell and told the servant to bring him some wine. After enjoying a few glasses of claret his senses grew dim and he fell asleep.

IV

Yegor Semyonych and Tanya had frequent quarrels and said nasty things to each other. One morning, after a squabble about something, Tanya burst into tears and went to her room. She didn't appear for lunch, or tea. At first Yegor Semyonych walked around solemnly and pompously, as if he wanted to make it known that he considered justice and order more important than anything else in the world. But he could not keep up the pose for long and lost heart. Sadly he wandered through the park, sighing the whole time, 'Ah, Good Lord, Good Lord!' and he did not eat a thing for dinner. Finally, full of guilt and remorse, he knocked on the locked door and called out timidly, 'Tanya! Tanya?'

A weak voice, drained by tears, but still determined, replied from behind the door, 'Leave me alone, I beg you.'

The anguish of the master and mistress was reflected all over the house, even in the gardeners. Kovrin was immersed in his interesting work, but in the end he too felt bored and embarrassed. Trying to dispel the prevailing unpleasant atmosphere, he decided to intervene and towards evening knocked at Tanya's door. She let him in.

'Come now, you should be ashamed!' he joked, looking in amazement at Tanya's tear-stained, mournful face that was covered in red blotches. 'Surely it's not as bad as all that? Now, now!'

'If you only knew how he torments me!' she said and copious, bitter tears welled from her large eyes. 'He's tormented the life out of me,' she went on, wringing her hands. 'I didn't say *anything* to him . . . nothing at all. I only said we don't need to keep on extra workers when . . . when we can engage day-labourers if we want to. You know, our gardeners have been standing idle for a whole week. That's all I said, but he shouted and said many insulting, deeply offensive things. Why?'

'Now, that's enough, enough,' Kovrin said, smoothing her hair. 'You've had your quarrel and a good cry, and that's enough. You must stop being angry now, it's not good . . . especially as he loves you so very much.'

'He's ruined my whole life,' Tanya continued, sobbing. 'All I hear is insults and abuse . . . He thinks there's no place for me in this house. Agreed. He's right. I'll leave this place tomorrow, get a job as a telegraphist . . . That's what I'll do.'

'Come now, there's no need to cry, Tanya. Please don't, my dear . . . You're both quick-tempered, easily upset, and you're both to blame. Come on, I'll make peace between you.'

Kovrin spoke with feeling, convincingly, but she kept on crying, her shoulders twitching and her hands clenched as if something really terrible had happened to her. He felt all the more sorry for her because, although her grief was nothing serious, she was suffering deeply. How little it took to make this creature unhappy all day long, for her whole life perhaps! As he comforted Tanya, Kovrin thought that he wouldn't find two people who loved him so much as Tanya and her father in a month of Sundays. Having lost his father and mother as a small child, but for these two, probably, he would never have known true affection until his dying day. He would never have known that simple, disinterested love that is felt only for those who are very close, for blood relations. And he felt that this weeping, trembling girl's nerves were reacting to his own half-sick, over-wrought nerves like iron to a magnet. He could never have loved a healthy, strong, rosy-cheeked woman, but that pale, weak, unhappy Tanya attracted him.

And he gladly stroked her hair and shoulders, pressed her hands and wiped away the tears ... Finally she stopped crying. For a long time she complained about her father and her hard, intolerable life in that house, imploring Kovrin to see things as she did. Then gradually, she began to smile and said sighing that God had given her *such* a bad character. In the end she laughed out loud, called herself a fool and ran out of the room.

Shortly afterwards, when Kovrin went into the garden, Yegor Semyonych and Tanya were strolling side by side along the path as if nothing had happened. They were both eating rye bread with salt, as they were hungry.

V

Pleased with his success as peacemaker, Kovrin went into the park. As he sat pondering on a bench he heard the clatter of carriages and a woman's laughter – guests had arrived. As the shadows of evening fell across the garden he heard the vague sounds of a violin, voices singing, which reminded him of the black monk. Where, in what country or on what planet was that optical absurdity wandering now?

Hardly had he recalled that legend, conjuring up the dark spectre he had seen in the rye field, when quite silently, without the slightest rustling, a man of medium height, his grey head uncovered, all in black, barefoot like a beggar, his black eyebrows sharply defined on his deathly white face, slipped out from behind the pine trees just opposite. Nodding his head welcomingly, this beggar or pilgrim silently came over to the bench and Kovrin could see it was the black monk. For a minute they both eyed each other – Kovrin in amazement, the monk in a friendly way, with that same rather crafty look.

'You're just a mirage,' Kovrin murmured. 'Why are you here, sitting still like that? It doesn't tally with the legend.'

'Never mind,' the monk answered softly after a brief pause, turning his face towards him. 'The legend, myself, the mirage are all products of your overheated imagination. I'm an apparition . . .'

'That means you don't exist?' Kovrin asked.

'Think what you like,' the monk said with a weak smile. 'I exist in your imagination, and your imagination is part of nature, so I exist in nature too.'

'You have a very aged, clever and extremely expressive face, as if you really have lived more than a thousand years,' Kovrin said. 'I didn't know my imagination could create such phenomena. But why are you looking at me so rapturously? Do you like me?'

'Yes. You're one of the few who are rightly called God's Chosen. You serve Eternal Truth. Your ideas, intentions, your amazing erudition, your whole life – all bear the divine, heavenly stamp, since they are devoted to the Rational and the Beautiful, that is, to the Eternal.'

'You mentioned "Eternal Truth" . . . But is that within men's reach, do they need it if there's no such thing as eternal life?'

'There *is* eternal life,' the monk said.

'Do you believe in immortality?'

'Yes, of course. A great, bright future awaits you human beings. And the more men there are like you on earth, the quicker will this future come about. Without men like you serving the highest principles, living intelligently and freely, humanity would be worthless. In the normal course of events it would have to wait a long time for its life upon earth to come to an end. But you will lead it into the Kingdom of Eternal Truth a few thousand years ahead of time – this is your noble service. You are the embodiment of God's blessing which has come to dwell among men.'

'But what is the purpose of eternal life?' asked Kovrin.

'Like any other kind of life – pleasure. True pleasure is knowledge, and eternal life will afford innumerable and inexhaustible sources of knowledge: this is the meaning of the saying, "In my Father's house are many mansions."'

'If you only knew how enjoyable it is listening to you!' Kovrin said, rubbing his hands with pleasure.

'I'm very pleased.'

'But I know one thing: when you've gone I'll start worrying whether you really do exist. You're a phantom, a hallucination. Does that mean I'm mentally ill, insane?'

'Even if that were so, why let it bother you? You're ill from overworking, you've worn yourself out. I'm trying to say that you've sacrificed your health for an idea and it won't be long before you sacrifice your very life to it. What could be better? All noble spirits blessed with gifts from on high have this as their aim.'

'If I *know* that I'm mentally ill, how can I have any faith in myself?'

'But how do you know that men of genius, in whom the whole world puts its faith, haven't seen ghosts too? Nowadays scientists say genius is akin to madness. My friend, only the mediocre, the common herd are healthy and normal. Thoughts about an age of neurosis, overwork, degeneracy and so on can seriously worry only

those for whom the purpose of life lies in the present –
that is, the common herd.'

'The Romans used to speak of *mens sana in corpore
sano.*'

'Not all that the Greeks and Romans said is true.
Heightened awareness, excitement, ecstasy – everything
that distinguishes prophets, poets, martyrs to an idea,
from ordinary people is hostile to man's animal side – I
mean, his physical health. I repeat: if you want to be
healthy and normal, go and join the herd.'

'It's strange the way you repeat things I think of myself
very often,' Kovrin said. 'It's as though you spied out and
eavesdropped on my most secret thoughts. But let's not
talk about me. What do you mean by Eternal Truth?'

The monk did not answer. Kovrin looked at him and
could not make out his face – its features had become
hazy and indistinct. Then the monk's head and arms
began to disappear. His torso merged with the bench
and the twilight shadows, and he vanished completely.

'The hallucination's over!' Kovrin said laughing. 'A
pity!'

He went back to the house happy and cheerful. The
monk's few words had flattered not his pride, but his very
soul, his whole being. To be one of the Chosen, to serve
Eternal Truth, to stand in the ranks of those who, a thousand years ahead of time, would make men worthy of the
Kingdom of God, thereby saving them from several thousand years of needless struggle, sin and suffering, to

surrender, to surrender everything – youth, strength, health – to an idea, to be ready to die for the common weal – what a noble, blissful destiny! The memory of his pure, chaste, hardworking past flashed through his mind; he remembered what he had learned, what he had taught others, and he decided that the monk had not been exaggerating.

As he went through the park he met Tanya. She was wearing a different dress now.

'So you're here,' she said. 'We've all been looking for you, looking everywhere . . . But what's the matter?' she asked in surprise, studying his radiant, glowing face. 'How strange you are, Andrey.'

'I'm contented, Tanya,' Kovrin said as he put his hands on her shoulders. 'I'm more than contented, I'm happy! Tanya, dear Tanya, you're such a likeable person! Dear Tanya, I'm so glad, so glad!'

He kissed both her hands passionately and went on, 'I've just experienced some bright, wonderful, divine moments. But I can't tell you everything, because you'd call me mad or disbelieve me. Let's talk about you. Dear, wonderful Tanya! I love you. I'm *used* to loving you now. Having you near me, meeting you ten times a day has become a spiritual necessity. I don't know how I will cope when I go home.'

'Well!' Tanya laughed. 'You'll forget about us in a couple of days. We're small fry and you're a great man.'

'No, let's be serious!' he said. 'I shall take you with me,

63

Tanya. Will you say yes? Will you come with me? Will you be mine?'

'Well!' Tanya said and felt like laughing again. But she could not and her face came out in red blotches. Her breath came faster and she quickly went away, not towards the house, but further into the park. 'I hadn't given it any thought . . . I hadn't thought . . .' she said, wringing her hands despairingly.

But Kovrin kept following her, still speaking with that same radiant, rapturous expression on his face, 'I want a love which will completely transport me, and only *you* can give me that love, Tanya! I'm happy, so happy!'

Quite stunned, she stooped, shrank and suddenly seemed to have aged ten years. But he found her beautiful and shouted out in delight, 'How beautiful she is!'

VI

When he heard from Kovrin that not only were they enamoured of each other, but that there was even going to be a wedding, Yegor Semyonych paced up and down for a long time, trying to conceal his excitement. His hands started shaking, his neck swelled up and turned crimson. He ordered his racing droshky to be harnessed and drove off somewhere. When Tanya saw him whipping the horses and pulling his cap almost onto his ears, she realized the kind of mood he was in, locked herself in her room and cried all day long.

The peaches and plums in the hothouses were already ripe. The packing and despatch of this delicate, temperamental cargo required a great deal of care, labour and trouble. Because of the very hot, dry summer, each tree needed watering, which involved a great deal of the gardeners' time. Swarms of caterpillars appeared, which the gardeners – even Yegor Semyonych and Tanya – squashed with their bare fingers, much to Kovrin's disgust. Besides this, they had to take orders for fruit and trees for the autumn and conduct an extensive correspondence. And at the most critical time, when no one seemed to have a moment to spare, the harvesting started and this took half the workforce away from the garden. Extremely sunburnt, worn-out and in a dreadful mood, Yegor Semyonych would tear off into the garden, then out into the fields, shouting that they were tearing him to pieces and that he was going to put a bullet in his head.

And now there were rows about the trousseau, to which the Pesotskys attached no little importance. The snipping of scissors, the rattle of sewing-machines, the fumes from the hot-irons, the tantrums of the dressmaker – a nervous, touchy woman – had everyone's head in a whirl in that household. And as ill luck would have it, guests turned up every day and had to be amused, fed, even put up for the night. But all this toil passed by unnoticed, as though in a mist. Tanya felt as if she had been caught quite unawares by love and happiness, although, from the age of fourteen, she had been somehow sure that Kovrin would marry her, and no one else. She was amazed, bewildered and could not believe what had happened. One moment she would feel such joy that she wanted to fly up into the clouds and offer prayers to God; another time she would suddenly remember that she would have to leave her little nest and part from her father in August; on another occasion the thought would come to her, God knows from where, that she was an insignificant, trivial sort of woman, unworthy of a great man like Kovrin, and she would go to her room, lock the door and cry bitterly for several hours. When they had visitors she would suddenly find Kovrin extremely handsome and think that all the women were in love with him and jealous of her. And her heart would fill with rapturous pride, as if she had conquered the whole world. But he only had to give some young woman a welcoming smile and she would tremble with jealousy, go to her room – and there would be tears again. These new feelings took complete hold of her, she helped her father as though she were a machine and was blind to peaches, caterpillars, workers, oblivious of how swiftly the time was passing.

Almost exactly the same thing was happening to Yegor Semyonych. He worked from morning till night, was always hurrying off somewhere, would boil over and lose his temper, but all this in some kind of magical half-sleep.

He seemed to be two different persons at once: one was the real Yegor Semyonych, listening to the head gardener Ivan Karlych's reports of things going wrong, flaring up and clutching his head in despair; the other was not the real Yegor Semyonych, a half-intoxicated person who would suddenly break off a conversation about business in the middle of a sentence, tap the head gardener on the shoulder and mutter, 'Whatever you say, good stock matters. His mother was an amazing, noble, brilliant woman. It was a pleasure looking at her kind, bright, pure face, the face of an angel. She was excellent at drawing, wrote poetry, spoke five languages, sang . . . The poor woman, God rest her soul, died of consumption.'

The unreal Yegor Semyonych would continue after a brief silence, 'When he was a boy, growing up in my house, he had the same angelic, bright, kind face. And his look, his movements and his conversation were like his mother's – gentle and refined. And as for his intellect, he always staggered us with his intellect. By the way, he didn't become an MA for nothing, oh no! But you wait and see, Ivan Karlych, what he'll be like in ten years' time! There'll be no touching him!'

But at this point the real Yegor Semyonych would suddenly take charge, pull a terrifying face, clutch his head and shout, 'The swines! They've polluted, fouled, frozen everything solid! The garden's ruined! It's finished!'

But Kovrin kept on working with his former enthusiasm and did not notice all the commotion around him.

Love only added fuel to the flames. After every meeting with Tanya he would return to his room feeling happy, exultant and would pick up a book or manuscript with the same passion with which he had just kissed Tanya and declared his love. What the black monk had told him about God's Chosen, Eternal Truth, humanity's glittering future and so on lent his work a special, remarkable significance and filled his heart with pride and awareness of his own outstanding qualities. Once or twice a week he met the black monk in the park or in the house, had a talk with him, but it did not frighten him. On the contrary, it delighted him, as he was now firmly convinced that these kinds of visions visited only the select few, only outstanding men who had dedicated themselves to an idea.

One day the monk appeared at dinner time and sat by the window in the dining-room. Kovrin was overjoyed and deftly started a conversation with Yegor Semyonych on a topic that the monk would very likely find interesting. The black visitor listened and nodded his head amiably. Yegor Semyonych and Tanya listened too, cheerfully smiling and without suspecting that Kovrin was speaking not to them, but to his hallucination.

The Fast of the Assumption came unnoticed and soon afterwards the wedding day, which, as Yegor Semyonych insisted, was celebrated with 'a great splash', that is to say, with senseless festivities that went on for two whole days. They got through three thousand roubles' worth of food and drink, but with that miserable hired band, the riotous toasts and scurrying servants, the noise and the crush, they did not appreciate the expensive wines, nor the startling delicacies that had been ordered from Moscow.

VII

One long winter's night Kovrin was reading a French novel in bed. Poor Tanya, who suffered from headaches in the evening as she wasn't used to town life, had long been asleep and was muttering something incoherent.

Three o'clock struck. Kovrin snuffed the candle and lay down. He remained with eyes closed for a long time, but he could not sleep, possibly because the bedroom was very hot and Tanya was talking in her sleep. At half past four he lit the candle again and this time he saw the black monk sitting in the armchair near the bed.

'Good evening,' the monk said. After a brief pause he asked, 'What are you thinking about now?'

'Fame,' Kovrin answered. 'I've just been reading a French novel about a young scholar who does stupid things and who's wasting away because of his longing for fame. This longing is something I can't understand.'

'That's because you're intelligent. You're indifferent to fame, it's a toy that doesn't interest you.'

'Yes, that's true.'

'Fame doesn't tempt you. What is flattering, or amusing, or edifying in having your name carved on a tombstone only for it to be rubbed off by time, gilding as well? Fortunately there are too many of you for humanity's weak memory to retain your names.'

'I understand that,' Kovrin agreed. 'And why should they be remembered? But let's talk about something else. Happiness, for example. What is happiness?'

When the clock struck five he was sitting on the bed, his feet dangling over the carpet. He turned to the monk and said, 'In antiquity, a certain happy man grew scared of his own good fortune in the end, it was so immense. So, to propitiate the Gods, he sacrificed his favourite ring. Do you know that I myself, like Polycrates, am getting rather uneasy about my own good fortune? It seems strange that from morning to night I feel only joy, it fills my whole being and stifles all other feelings. As for sorrow, sadness or boredom, I just don't know what they are. Here I am, unable to sleep, suffering from insomnia, but I'm not bored. Seriously, I'm beginning to wonder what it all means.'

'But why?' the monk said in astonishment. 'Is joy something supernatural? Shouldn't it be looked on as man's normal state? The higher man's intellectual and moral development, the freer he is and the more pleasure life gives him. Socrates, Diogenes and Marcus Aurelius experienced joy, not sadness. And the Apostle says, "Rejoice evermore." So rejoice and be happy.'

'But supposing the Gods suddenly became angry?' Kovrin said jokingly and burst out laughing. 'If they were to take my comforts away and make me freeze and starve I don't think I would like that.'

Meanwhile Tanya had woken up and she looked at her husband in horror and bewilderment. He was talking to the armchair, laughing and gesticulating. His eyes shone and there was something peculiar in his laughter.

'Andrey, who are you talking to?' she asked, clutching the hand he had held out to the monk. 'Andrey, who is it?'

'What? Who?' Kovrin said, taken aback. 'Well, to *him* . . . He's sitting over there,' he said, pointing at the black monk.

'There's no one here . . . no one! Andrey, you're ill!' Tanya embraced her husband and pressed herself against him, as if to protect him from ghosts, and covered his eyes with her hand. 'You're ill!' she sobbed, shaking all over. 'Forgive me, my dearest, but for some time now I've noticed something's wrong with you. You're sick in your mind, Andrey . . .'

Her trembling infected him as well. He looked once more at the armchair, which was empty now and felt a sudden weakness in his arms and legs. This frightened him and he started to dress.

'It's nothing, Tanya, nothing,' he muttered, trembling. 'But to tell the truth, I am a little unwell . . . it's time I admitted it.'

'I noticed it some time ago . . . and Papa did too,' she

said, trying to hold back her sobs. 'You talk to yourself, you smile so strangely . . . you're not sleeping. Oh, good God, good God, save us!' she said in horror. 'But don't be afraid, Andrey dear, don't be afraid. For God's sake don't be afraid . . .'

She began to dress too. Only now, as he looked at her, did Kovrin fully realize how dangerous his position was, only now did he understand the meaning of the black monk and his talks with him. He was quite convinced now that he was insane.

Both of them got dressed, without understanding why, and went into the ballroom, she first and he following. And there stood Yegor Semyonych (he was staying with them and had been awakened by the sobbing) in his dressing-gown, with a candle in his hand.

'Don't be afraid, Andrey,' Tanya said, shaking as though in a fever. 'Don't be afraid . . . Papa, it will pass . . . it will pass . . .'

Kovrin could not speak, he was so upset. He wanted to tell his father-in-law, just for a joke, 'Please congratulate me, I think I've gone mad . . .', but all he could do was move his lips and smile bitterly.

At nine in the morning they put his greatcoat and furs on, wrapped a shawl round him and took him in a carriage to the doctor's. He began a course of treatment.

VIII

Summer had come and the doctor ordered him into the country. Kovrin was better now, had stopped seeing the black monk and it only remained for him to get his strength back. Living with his father-in-law in the country, he drank a lot of milk, worked only two hours a day, and did not drink or smoke.

On the eve of Elijah's Day evening service was held in the house. When the lay reader handed the priest the censer, the enormous old ballroom smelt like a graveyard. Kovrin grew bored. He went out into the garden, wandered about without noticing the gorgeous flowers, sat down on a bench, and then strolled through the park. When he reached the river he went down the slope and stood looking thoughtfully at the water. The gloomy pines with their shaggy roots which had seen him here the previous year looking so young, joyful and lively, no longer talked in whispers, but stood motionless and dumb, as though they did not recognize him. And in fact his hair had been cut short, it was no longer beautiful, he walked sluggishly and his face had grown fuller and paler since the previous summer.

He crossed the footbridge to the other side. Where rye had been growing last year were rows of reaped oats. The sun had already set and a broad red glow burned on the horizon, a sign that it would be windy next day. It was quiet. Looking hard in the direction where the black monk had first appeared last year, Kovrin stood for about twenty minutes until the evening glow began to fade.

When he returned to the house, feeling listless and dissatisfied, the service was over. Yegor Semyonych and Tanya were sitting on the terrace steps drinking tea. They were discussing something, but suddenly became silent when they saw Kovrin, and he guessed from their expressions that they had been talking about him.

'Well, I think it's time for your milk,' Tanya told her husband.

'No, it's not,' he answered, sitting on the lowest step. 'Drink it yourself, I don't want any.'

Tanya anxiously exchanged glances with her father and said quietly, 'But you yourself said the milk does you a lot of good!'

'Yes, a lot of good!' Kovrin replied, grinning. 'I congratulate you – since Friday I've put on another pound.' He firmly clasped his head and said in an anguished voice, 'Why, why did you try to cure me? All those bromides, idleness, warm baths, supervision, the cowardly fear with every mouthful, every step. All this will finally turn me into a complete idiot. I was going out of my mind, I had megalomania, but I was bright and cheerful, even happy. I was interesting and original. Now I've grown more rational and stable, but I'm just like everyone else, a nobody. Life bores me . . . Oh, how cruelly you've treated me! I did have hallucinations, but did they harm anyone? Whom did they harm, that's what I'd like to know?'

'God knows what you're talking about!' Yegor Semyonych sighed. 'It's downright boring listening to you.'

'Then don't listen.'

Kovrin found other people's presence, especially Yegor Semyonych's, irritating and he would answer him drily, coldly, rudely even; and he could not look at him without a feeling of hatred and mockery, which embarrassed Yegor Semyonych, who would cough guiltily, although he didn't feel he was in the least to blame. Unable to understand why their friendly, loving relationship had changed so suddenly, Tanya pressed close to her father and looked him anxiously in the eye. She wanted to understand, but she could not, and she could only see that with every day relations were getting worse, that her father had aged considerably recently, while her husband had become irritable, moody, quarrelsome and uninteresting. No longer could she laugh and sing, she ate nothing at mealtimes, and lay awake whole nights expecting something terrible. She went through such torture that once she lay in a faint from lunch until the evening. During the service she thought that her father was crying and now, when the three of them sat on the terrace, she endeavoured not to think about it.

'How fortunate Buddha, Muhammad or Shakespeare were in not being treated by kind-hearted relatives for ecstasy and inspiration!' Kovrin said. 'If Muhammad had taken potassium bromide for his nerves, had worked only two hours a day and drunk milk, then that remarkable man would have left as much to posterity as his dog. In the long run doctors and kind relatives will turn humanity into a lot of morons. Mediocrity will pass for genius and civilization will perish. If only you knew,' Kovrin added with annoyance, 'how grateful I am to you!'

He was absolutely infuriated and quickly got up and went into the house, in case he said too much. It was quiet and the smell of tobacco flowers and jalap drifted in from the garden through the open windows. Green patches of moonlight lay on the floor in the huge dark ballroom and on the grand piano. Kovrin recalled the joys of the previous summer, when there was that same smell of jalap, and the moon had shone through the windows. Trying to recapture that mood he hurried to his study, lit a strong cigar and told a servant to bring him some wine. But the cigar left a bitter, disgusting taste and the wine tasted differently from last year: these were the effects of having given up the habit. The cigar and two mouthfuls of wine made his head go round, he had palpitations, for which he had to take potassium bromide.

Before she went to bed Tanya told him, 'Father adores you. You're cross with him about something and this is killing him. Just look, he's ageing by the hour, not by the day. I beg you, Andrey, for God's sake, for the sake of your late father, for the sake of my peace of mind, *please* be nice to him!'

'I can't and I won't!'

'But why not?' Tanya asked, trembling all over. 'Tell me, why not?'

'Because I don't like him, that's all,' Kovrin said nonchalantly, with a shrug of the shoulders. 'But let's not talk about him, he's *your* father.'

'I just can't understand, I really can't!' Tanya said, clutching her temples and staring fixedly at something. 'Something incomprehensible and horrible is going on in this house. You've changed, you're not your normal self. A clever, remarkable man like you losing your temper over trifles, getting mixed up in petty squabbles . . . These little things worry you and sometimes I'm simply amazed, I just can't believe it's really you.' Then she continued, frightened of her own words and kissing his hands, 'Now, now, don't be angry, don't be angry. You are a clever man, and a good man. You will be fair to Father, he's so kind.'

'He's not kind, only smug. Music-hall clowns like your father, bounteous old cranks, with their well-fed, smug faces, used to touch and amuse me once in stories, farces and in real life. But now I find them repugnant. They're egotists to the marrow. What I find most disgusting is their being so well fed, with that optimism that comes from a full belly. They're just like oxen or wild pigs.'

Tanya sat on the bed and lay her head on the pillow. 'This is sheer torture,' she said and from her voice it was plain that she was utterly exhausted and that she found it hard to speak. 'Not a single moment's peace since winter . . . It's so terrible. Oh God, I feel shocking!'

'Yes, of course I'm the monster and you and your Papa are the sweet innocents. Of course!'

His face seemed ugly and unpleasant to Tanya. Hatred and that mocking expression did not suit him. And she had in fact noticed before that there was something lacking in his face, as if that had changed too since his hair was cut short. She wanted to say something to hurt him, but immediately she became aware of this hostile feeling she grew frightened and left the bedroom.

IX

Kovrin was awarded a professorship. His inaugural lecture was fixed for 2 December and a notice announcing it was put up in the university corridor. But on the appointed day he cabled the dean, informing him he was not well enough to lecture.

He had a haemorrhage in the throat. He would spit blood, but twice a month there was considerable loss of blood, which left him extremely weak and drowsy. The illness did not frighten him particularly, since he knew his late mother had lived with exactly the same disease for ten years or more. And the doctors assured him it was not dangerous, and merely advised him not to get excited, to lead a regular life and to talk as little as possible.

In January the lecture was again cancelled for the same reason and in February it was too late to start the course, which had to be postponed until the following year.

He no longer lived with Tanya, but with another woman two years older than he was and who cared for him as though he were a child. His state of mind was calm, submissive. He eagerly gave in to her and when Barbara (his mistress's name) decided to take him to the Crimea he agreed, although he expected no good to come from the trip.

They reached Sevastopol one evening and rested at a hotel before going on to Yalta the next day. They were both exhausted from the journey. Barbara drank some tea, went to bed and soon fell asleep. But Kovrin did not go to bed. Before he had left home – an hour before setting off for the station – he had received a letter from Tanya and had decided not to open it. It was now in one of his coat pockets and the thought of it had a disagreeable, unsettling effect on him. In the very depths of his heart he now considered his marriage to Tanya had been a mistake, and was pleased he had finally broken with her. The memory of that woman who had ended up as a walking skeleton and in whom everything seemed to have died – except for those large, clever, staring eyes – this memory aroused only pity in him and annoyance with himself. The writing on the envelope reminded him how unjust and cruel he had been two years ago, how he had taken revenge on others for his spiritual

79

emptiness, his boredom, his loneliness, his dissatisfaction with life.

In this respect he remembered how he had once torn his dissertation and all the articles written during his illness into shreds and thrown them out of the window, the scraps of paper fluttering in the breeze, catching on trees and flowers. In every line he saw strange, utterly unfounded claims, enthusiasm run riot, audacity and megalomania, which had made him feel as if he were reading a description of his own vices. But when the last notebook had been torn up and had flown through the window, he felt for some reason bitterly annoyed: he had gone to his wife and told her many unpleasant things. God, how he had tormented her! Once, when he wanted to hurt his wife, he told her that her father had played a most distasteful role in their romance, having asked him if he would marry her. Yegor Semyonych happened to hear this and rushed into the room speechless with despair; all he could do was stamp his feet and make a strange bellowing noise, as if he had lost the power of speech, while Tanya looked at her father, gave a heart-rending shriek and fainted. It was an ugly scene.

All this came to mind at the sight of the familiar handwriting. Kovrin went out onto the balcony. The weather was warm and calm, and he could smell the sea. The magnificent bay reflected the moon and the lights, and its colour was hard to describe. It was a delicate, soft blending of dark-blue and green; in places the water was like blue vitriol, in others the moonlight seemed to have taken on material substance and filled the bay instead of water. But what a harmony of colour, what a peaceful, calm and ennobling mood reigned over all!

The windows were most probably open in the room below, beneath the balcony, as he could hear women's voices and laughter quite distinctly. Someone was having a party, it seemed.

Kovrin forced himself to open the letter, returned to his room and read: 'Father has just died. I owe that to you, as you killed him. Our garden is going to rack and ruin – strangers are running it – that's to say, what poor father feared so much has come about. I owe this to you as well. I hate you with all my heart and hope you'll soon be dead. Oh, how I'm suffering! An unbearable pain is burning inside me. May you be damned! I took you for an outstanding man, for a genius, I loved you, but you turned out a madman . . .'

Kovrin could not read any more, tore the letter up and threw it away. He was seized by a feeling of anxiety that was very close to terror. Barbara was sleeping behind a screen and he could hear her breathing. From the ground floor came women's voices and laughter, but he felt that besides himself there wasn't a living soul in the whole hotel. He was terrified because the unhappy, broken-hearted Tanya had cursed him in her letter and had wished for his death. He glanced at the door, as if fearing that the unknown force which had wrought such havoc in his life and in the lives of those near and dear over the last two years might come into the room and take possession of him again.

He knew from experience that the best cure for shattered nerves is work. One should sit down at a table and force oneself at all costs to concentrate on one idea, no matter what. From his red briefcase he took out a notebook in which he had sketched out a plan for a short work he had considered compiling in case he was bored doing nothing in the Crimea. He sat at the table and busied himself with the plan, and it seemed his calm, resigned, detached state of mind was returning. The notebook and plan even stimulated him to meditate on the world's vanity. He thought how much life demands in return for those insignificant or very ordinary blessings that it can bestow. For example, to receive a university chair in one's late thirties, to be a run-of-the-mill professor, expounding in turgid, boring, ponderous language commonplace ideas that were not even original, in brief, to achieve the status of a third-rate scholar he, Kovrin, had had to study fifteen years – working day and night – suffer severe mental illness, experience a broken marriage and do any number of stupid, unjust things that were best forgotten. Kovrin realized quite clearly now that he was a nobody and eagerly accepted the fact since, in his opinion, every man should be content with what he is.

The plan would have calmed his nerves, but the sight of the shiny white pieces of letter on the floor stopped him concentrating. He got up from the table, picked up the pieces and threw them out of the window, but a light breeze blew in from the sea and scattered them over the windowsill. Once again he was gripped by that restless feeling, akin to panic, and he began to think that there was no one else besides him in the whole hotel . . . He went out onto the balcony. The bay, which seemed to be alive, looked at him with its many sky-blue, dark-blue, turquoise and flame-coloured eyes and beckoned him. It was truly hot and humid, and a bathe would not have come amiss. A violin began to play on the ground floor, under his balcony, and two female voices softly sang a song he knew. It was about some young girl, sick in her mind, who heard mysterious sounds one night in her garden and thought it must be a truly divine harmony, incomprehensible to us mortals . . . Kovrin caught his breath, he felt twinges of sadness in his heart and a wonderful, sweet, long-forgotten gladness quivered in his heart.

A tall black column like a whirlwind or tornado appeared on the far side of the bay. With terrifying speed it moved over the water towards the hotel, growing smaller and darker as it approached, and Kovrin barely had time to move out of its path . . . Barefoot, arms folded over chest, with a bare grey head and black eyebrows, the monk floated past and stopped in the middle of the room.

'Why didn't you trust me?' he asked reproachfully, looking affectionately at Kovrin. 'If you had trusted me then, when I told you that you were a genius, you wouldn't have spent these two years so miserably, so unprofitably.'

Kovrin believed now that he was one of God's Chosen, and a genius, and he vividly recollected all his previous conversations with the black monk; he wanted to speak, but the blood welled out of his throat onto his chest. Not knowing what to do, he drew his hands over his chest and his shirt cuffs became soaked with blood. He wanted to call Barbara, who was sleeping behind the screen, and with a great effort murmured, 'Tanya!'

He fell on the floor, lifted himself on his arms and called again, 'Tanya!'

He called on Tanya, on the great garden with its gorgeous flowers sprinkled with dew, he called on the park, the pines with their shaggy roots, the rye field, his wonderful learning, his youth, his daring, his joy; he called on life, which had been so beautiful. On the floor near his face, he saw a large pool of blood and was too weak now to say one word, but an ineffable, boundless happiness flooded his whole being. Beneath the balcony they were playing a serenade, and at the same time the black monk whispered to him that he was a genius and that he was dying only because his weak human body had lost its balance and could no longer serve to house a genius. When Barbara woke and came out from behind the screen Kovrin was dead and a blissful smile was frozen on his face.

Anna Round the Neck

I

Nothing was served after the wedding, not even light snacks. The bride and groom drank a glass of champagne, changed and drove off to the station. Instead of celebrating with a gay ball and supper, instead of music and dancing, they were going to a monastery a hundred and sixty miles away. Many of the guests approved, as Modeste Alekseyevich was a high-ranking official, wasn't so young any more, and a noisy reception might appear out of place. And in any case it's boring having music when a fifty-two-year-old civil servant marries a girl barely turned eighteen. Moreover, the guests said that a highly principled man like Modeste Alekseyevich must have organized the monastery trip to make it quite clear to his young wife that even in marriage he gave pride of place to religion and morality.

A crowd of office colleagues and relatives went to see them off and stood at the station, glasses in hand, waiting to cheer when the train left. Peter Leontyevich, the bride's father, in top-hat and schoolmaster's tail-coat, already

85

drunk and looking very pale, kept going up to the window of the carriage with a champagne glass and pleading with his daughter, 'Annie dear! Anne! I'd like to say just *one* word!'

Anne leant out of the window and he whispered some incomprehensible words, smothering her with alcohol fumes as he blew into her ear and made the sign of the cross over her face, bosom and hands. His breath came in short gasps and tears glistened in his eyes. Anne's schoolboy brothers, Peter and Andrew, tugged at his tail-coat from behind and whispered in embarrassment, 'That's enough, Papa, please stop!'

When the train started Anne saw her father running after them, staggering and spilling his wine. His face looked so pathetic, kind, guilty. 'Hoo-ooray!' he shouted.

The couple were alone now. Modeste looked round the compartment, put the luggage on the rack and sat smiling opposite his wife. He was a civil servant of medium height, rather round and plump, and very well fed. He had long side-whiskers (but no moustache) and his round clean-shaven pointed chin looked like a heel. The most striking feature in that face was the absence of a moustache, with a freshly-shaven bare patch instead, which gradually merged into two fat cheeks that wobbled like jellies. He had a dignified bearing, rather sluggish movements and gentle manners.

'At this moment in time I cannot but recall a certain event,' he said, smiling. 'When Kosorotov received the

Order of St Anne, second class, five years ago, he called on His Excellency to thank him. His Excellency used the following expression: "So now you've got three Annes, one in your buttonhole and two round your neck." I should explain that Kosorotov's wife had just come back to him – she was an irritable, empty-headed woman called Anne. I hope when *I* receive the Order of St Anne, second class, His Excellency will have no cause to make the same comment.'

His tiny eyes filled with a smile and Anne smiled too, disturbed at the thought that any moment this man might kiss her with his fat moist lips – and she wouldn't be able to say no. The smooth movements of his plump body frightened her and she felt terrified, disgusted.

He stood up and without hurrying took off the ribbon from round his neck, his tail-coat and waist-coat and put his dressing-gown on.

'That's better,' he said as he sat beside her.

She recalled the excruciating wedding service when she had thought that the priest, the guests and everyone in the church were looking at her sadly, asking themselves *why* an attractive girl like her was marrying an elderly, boring man. Earlier that morning she had felt delighted that everything had turned out so well, but during the service – and as she sat in the train now – she felt guilty, cheated and foolish. It was all very well having a rich husband, but she still didn't have any money. The wedding dress hadn't been paid for and that morning she could tell by the look on her father's and brothers' faces – when they had seen her off – that they didn't have a kopek between them. Would they have anything to eat that evening? Or the next? For some reason she began to think that her father and brothers would go hungry now she had gone, and would be sitting at home grieving as they had done the first evening after they had buried Mother.

'Oh, I'm *so* unhappy!' she thought. 'Why am I so unhappy?'

With the clumsiness one might expect from a respectable man who had no experience of women, Modeste kept touching her waist and patting her shoulder, but she could only think about money, about her mother and her death, after which her father, an art master at the high school, had taken to drink, so that they really began to feel the pinch. The boys had no boots or galoshes, the father was always in court, and the bailiffs came and put a distraint on the furniture. What a disgrace that had been! Anne had to look after her drunken father, darn her brothers' socks and go shopping. Whenever she was complimented on her looks, her youth and refined manners, she felt the whole world could see her cheap hat and the patches in her shoes which she had stained with ink. And there were tears at night and the nagging, unsettling thought that any day Father might be dismissed for drinking, that the blow would be too much for him and that he would die too. But some ladies – friends of the family – got busy and tried to find a husband for her. And in no time this Modeste Alekseyevich turned up, a man who was neither young nor good-looking, but he did have money – about a hundred thousand in the bank and a family estate which he let to a tenant. He was a gentleman of high principles, on good terms with His Excellency, and he only had to lift a finger to get a note from him for the headmaster or even the education committee and Peter Leontyevich would not lose his job.

While she was brooding over these details, a sudden burst of music and sound of voices came through the window. The train had reached a halt along the line. Two people in the crowd on the other side of the platform had struck up a lively tune on an accordion and a cheap squeaky violin, while from beyond the tall birches, poplars and moonlit country villas came the sound of a military band: most probably there was a dance at one of the villas. The resident holiday-makers and the day-trippers from town, who had come to enjoy the fine weather and fresh air, were strolling along the platform. Artynov was there – he owned all the holiday area and he was a rich, tall, stout man, with dark brown hair, bulging eyes and a face like an Armenian's. He was wearing a very strange outfit – an open-necked shirt, high boots with spurs and a black cloak that hung down from his shoulders and touched the ground like the train of a dress. Following him were two wolf-hounds with sharp, lowered muzzles.

Although the tears still glistened in Anne's eyes, now she forgot all about her mother, money and her wedding, and she smiled cheerfully as she shook familiar school-boys' and officers' hands with a quick: 'Hello! How are you?'

She went out on to the small platform at the end of the carriage and stood in the moonlight, so that they could all have a full view of her in her magnificent new dress and hat.

'Why are we stopping here?' she asked.

'It's a loop-line,' came the answer. 'They're waiting for the mail train to pass through.'

Noticing that Artynov was looking at her, she blinked coquettishly and started speaking out loud in French – the beautiful sound of her own voice, the music from the band, the moon's reflection in the pond, the fact that she had claimed Artynov's close attention (he was a notorious ladies' man and society darling, and was giving her hungry, inquisitive looks) – all of this, combined with the general mood of festivity, brought a surge of joy to her heart. When the train moved off and her officer friends had given her a farewell salute, she was already humming a polka, which the military band, roaring away somewhere behind the trees, sent flying after her. She returned to her compartment feeling that the stop at that country station had proved beyond doubt that now she could not fail to be happy, in spite of everything.

The couple spent two days at the monastery, then

returned to town to live in the flat provided by the author-
ities. When Modeste had gone off to work, Anne would
play the piano or cry with boredom, or lie down on the
couch and read novels or look at fashion magazines.
Modeste would eat a large dinner and talk about politics,
appointments, transfers and decorations, about hard
work not hurting anyone, about family life being a duty
and not a pleasure; and he maintained that if one took
care of the kopeks, the roubles would look after themselves and that religion and morality were the most
important things in life.

'Every man should have responsibilities,' he would say,
clenching his knife in his fist like a sword.

Anne would become so frightened, listening to all this,
that she couldn't eat and she would usually leave the table
hungry. Her husband would normally have a rest after
dinner and snore loudly, while she went off to see her
family. Her father and brothers would give her strange
looks as though – just before she arrived – they had been
condemning her for marrying that terrible bore, a man
she didn't love, for his money. For them the rustle of her
dress, the bracelets she wore, the way she looked like a
fine lady now, were inhibiting and insulting. They were
embarrassed by her visits and they just did not know
what to talk about. She would sit down and join them in
cabbage soup, porridge, or potatoes fried in mutton fat
reeking of candle-grease. Peter Leontyevich's hand would
shake as he filled his glass from the decanter and drink

rapidly and greedily, and with obvious disgust; then he would take a second, then a third. Peter and Andrew, skinny, pale-faced boys with large eyes, would take the decanter away and exclaim in despair, 'You mustn't, Papa . . . you've had enough.'

And Anne would grow anxious as well and she would plead with him to stop. This made him flare up, bang his fist on the table and shout, 'I *won't* be told what to do! Street urchins! And *you* little slut! I'll kick you out, the lot of you!'

But his weak, kind voice gave no one cause for alarm. After dinner he would usually smarten himself up: pale-faced, with his chin cut from shaving, craning his thin neck, he would stand a whole half-hour in front of the mirror trying to make himself look smart, combing his hair, twirling his black moustache, sprinkling himself with perfume or tying a bow-tie. Then he would put on his gloves and top-hat and go out to do some private coaching. If it was a holiday, he would stay at home and paint or play the harmonium, making it grunt and groan. He tried to squeeze beautiful melodies out of it, humming a bass accompaniment or losing his temper with the boys: 'Savages! Wretches! You've ruined it!'

In the evenings Anne's husband would play cards with colleagues who lived in the same government block. Their wives used to come along with them. They were ugly, tastelessly dressed, terribly coarse, and they filled the flat with malicious scandal-mongering that was as ugly and vulgar as themselves. Sometimes Modeste would take Anne to the theatre. In the intervals he made sure she kept close by him and would walk along the corridors and around the foyer holding her arm. After exchanging bows with someone he would whisper quickly, 'A senior government official,' or 'He's got money . . . has his own house . . .'

Anne would long for something sweet as they passed the bar. She loved chocolate and apple pie, but she didn't have any money and was too shy to ask her husband. He would take a pear, press it and ask hesitantly, 'How much?'

'Twenty-five kopeks.'

'Well, really!' he would say, replacing it.

As it was awkward leaving the bar without buying any-thing, he would ask for some soda-water and finish a whole bottle off himself, which made his eyes water. At these moments Anne hated him.

Another time he would suddenly turn bright red and hurriedly say, 'Bow to that old lady.'

'But I don't know her.'

'It doesn't matter, she's the wife of the manager of the local revenue office. Bow, I'm telling you,' he would growl insistently. 'Your head won't fall off!'

So Anne would bow and her head didn't fall off. But it was an ordeal, just the same. She did everything her husband wanted and was furious with herself for letting him make such an absolute fool of her. She had married him for his money and now she was worse off than before. Her father, at least, used to give her twenty-kopek pieces, but now she didn't get anything. She could not bring herself to take any money when he wasn't there or ask for some as she was frightened of her husband, frightened to death, in fact.

She felt that she had *always* had this fear of him. When she was a child, she invariably thought of the headmaster of the local high school as a most awe-inspiring, terrifying force, advancing on her like a storm-cloud or a railway engine that was about to run her over. Another such power – always a subject for discussion in the family and whom they feared as well – was His Excellency. And there were about a dozen lesser fry, including stern, smooth-shaven, unmerciful schoolmasters; and finally, along had come that Modeste Alekseyevich, a man of high principles, who even looked like the headmaster. In her imagination all these forces merged together and took the form of an enormous, terrifying polar bear, advancing on the weak and on those who had gone astray – like her father – and she was too scared to protest, would force herself to smile and pretend to be pleased when they roughly caressed her or dirtied her with their embraces.

Once – and only once – Peter Leontyevich dared to ask if he could borrow fifty-five roubles to settle a particularly nasty debt, but what an ordeal it was! 'All right, I'll let you have it,' Modeste said, after a moment's deliberation, 'but I'm warning you. That's all the help you'll get from me until you stop drinking. This weakness is quite disgraceful for a man in government service. I must remind you of the universally recognized fact that this vice has been the ruin of many able men who, had they only been able to control themselves, might eventually have come to occupy high positions.'

And there followed rambling periods, one after the other: 'in so far as' or 'if we take *that* as a starting-point' or 'in view of the aforesaid', all of which humiliated poor Peter Leontyevich and made him die for a drink.

The boys, who usually had holes in their boots and worn-out trousers when they visited Anne, were also subjected to these lectures.

'*Every* man should have responsibilities,' Modeste would tell them. But he didn't give them any money. However, he presented Anne with rings, bracelets and brooches, and told her that they should be kept for a rainy day. Often he would unlock her chest of drawers to check if anything was missing.

II

Meanwhile winter had set in. Long before Christmas it was announced in the local paper that the usual winter ball would 'take place' on 29 December at the Assembly Rooms. Every evening after cards, Modeste Alekseyevich would get excited and have whispering sessions with civil servants' wives while he anxiously glanced at Anne. Then he would pace from corner to corner for a long time, deep in thought. Finally, late one evening, he stopped in front of Anne and said, 'You must get a dress for the ball. Do you understand? But first consult Marya Grigoryevna and Natalya Kuzminishna.'

And he gave her a hundred roubles, which she took. But when it came to ordering the dress she wouldn't consult anyone, talked only to her father and tried to visualize how her mother would have dressed for the ball. Her mother had always dressed in the latest fashion and had taken great pains with Anne, making sure she was dressed elegantly, like a doll, and taught her to speak French and dance an excellent mazurka (before her marriage she had been a governess for five years). Like her mother, she knew how to turn an old dress into a new one, wash her gloves with benzine, hire jewels and – just like her mother – flutter her eyelids, roll her 'r's, strike beautiful poses, go into raptures when the occasion called for it, or look sad and mysterious. She had her dark hair and eyes and nervous temperament from her mother and the habit of making herself look pretty the whole time from her father.

When Modeste Alekseyevich came into her room half an hour before they left for the ball to tie his St Anne ribbon round his neck in front of the full-length mirror, he was enchanted by her beauty and the glitter of her new gossamer-like dress, and he smugly combed his whiskers and said, 'What a beauty I've got . . . really! Just look at you, my dearest Anne!' His voice suddenly became solemn as he went on, 'I've made you happy and tonight you can make *me* happy. Introduce yourself to His Excellency's wife, I beg you! For heaven's sake! She can help me get a senior position!'

They drove off to the ball and arrived at the Assembly Rooms; at the entrance there was a porter. The hall was full of clothes-racks, scurrying footmen and ladies in low-necked dresses shielding themselves from the draught with their fans. The place smelt of soldiers and gas lights. As Anne went up the staircase on her husband's arm she heard music and caught a glimpse of herself in an enormous mirror lit by many lamps. Then the joy welled up in her heart and she felt she would be happy – as she had been on that moonlit night at the railway halt. She bore herself proudly, confidently feeling for the first time that she was no longer a little girl, but a lady now, copying her late mother's walk and manner. And – for the first time in her life – she felt rich and free. She didn't feel at all tied down having her husband with her: she had already instinctively guessed that the company of an elderly husband didn't in the least lower her in anyone's eyes. On the contrary, it stamped her with that tantalizing mysteriousness adored by men. The orchestra was already roaring away and dancing had started in the large ballroom. After that government flat, Anne felt overcome in a world of light, colour, music and noise, and she glanced around the ballroom thinking how wonderful it all was. At once she picked out all the people in the crowd she had met at parties or on walks – officers, teachers, lawyers, civil servants, landowners, His Excellency, Artynov, society ladies in their very best dresses with plunging necklines – some beautiful and others ugly – already in position at the stands and stalls of the charity bazaar in aid of the poor. A huge officer with epaulettes (she had met him in the Old Kiev Road when she was a schoolgirl and couldn't remember his name now) seemed to loom up out of thin air and invited her to the waltz. She flew from her husband and felt she was sailing in a boat during a violent storm – while her husband remained behind on the distant shore. She danced the waltz, polka and quadrille with fire and enthusiasm, moving from one partner to the other, intoxicated by the music and the noise, mixing Russian with French, rolling her 'r's, laughing, without a thought for her husband or indeed anyone or anything. She had scored a success with the men – there was no doubt about that – and it wasn't really surprising. Breathless with excitement, she feverishly pressed her fan between her hands and wanted to drink. Her father, in a crumpled tail-coat that smelt of benzine, went up to her with a plate of pink ice-cream.

'You look enchanting,' he said, eyeing her delightedly, 'and I've never felt as sorry as I do now that you rushed into that marriage ... Why? I know you did it for us, but . . .' He pulled out a small bundle of notes with trembling hands and added, 'I was paid for a lesson today so I can repay your husband.'

She thrust the plate into his hands as she was grabbed by someone and whirled away from him; over her partner's shoulders she caught a glimpse of her father, who slid over the parquet floor, clasped a lady in his arms and tore around the room with her.

'He's so nice when he's sober!' she thought.

She danced a mazurka with the huge officer again. He moved across the floor very solemnly, ponderously, like a piece of meat in uniform, just turning his shoulder and chest and hardly shifting his feet – he didn't really want to dance at all. But she flitted around him, teasing him with her beauty and her bare neck. Her eyes burnt with desire, her movements were passionate, but her partner grew more and more cool towards her, holding his hand out graciously like a king bestowing a favour.

'Bravo, bravo!' shouted some onlookers.

But gradually he gave in. He was revitalized, very excited and spellbound by her. He became really animated and started moving easily, like a young man, while she merely moved her shoulders with an artful look, as though she were the queen and he the slave. Now she thought everyone was looking at them and dying with envy. The enormous officer hardly had time to thank her when the crowd suddenly parted and the men curiously stiffened up, their arms at their sides. It was all because

His Excellency was coming over in his tail-coat – with two stars on his chest. There was no doubt about it, His Excellency was heading for *her*, as he was staring straight at her with a sugary smile on his face – he always did this when he saw a pretty woman.

'Absolutely *delighted*. Really delighted!' he began. 'I'll have to lock your husband up for hiding his treasure for so long. I've a message from my wife,' he continued, offering his hand. 'You must help us ... Hm, yes ... They should award you a prize for beauty as they do in America ... Hm ... My wife is dying to meet you.'

He led her over to a stall, to an old lady whose enormous chin was so out of proportion to the rest of her face it looked as if she had a large stone in her mouth.

'Please come and help us,' she said in a twanging voice. 'Every pretty woman helps us with the charity bazaar and you're the only one who seems content just to have a good time. Why don't you come and help!'

She left and Anne took her place next to a silver samovar and some tea cups. Immediately she did a roaring trade. She wouldn't take less than a rouble for a cup of tea and she made the huge officer drink three cups. Artynov came over – he was a rich man with bulging eyes and who suffered from shortness of breath. He wasn't sporting that peculiar costume which Anne had seen him wearing during the summer, but wore a tail-coat like everyone else. Without taking his eyes off Anne, he drank a glass of champagne, for which he paid a hundred roubles. Then he drank some tea and gave another hundred – all this without saying a word, and breathing like an asthmatic. Anne coaxed her customers and took their money, quite convinced that these people derived only the greatest pleasure from her smiles and glances. Now she realized that *this* was the life she was born for, this noisy, brilliant life of music, laughter, dancing and admirers, and her earlier fears of that force which was bearing down on her, threatening to crush her, seemed quite comical. She was afraid of nobody now and only regretted that her mother was not there with her to share in her success.

Her father, white-faced, but still steady on his feet, came over to her stall and asked for a glass of brandy. Anne blushed, frightened he might make some indecent remark (she was ashamed enough of having such a pale, ordinary father). But he merely drank his brandy, threw ten roubles down from his bundle and solemnly walked away without saying a word. A little later she saw him dancing the *grand rond* with his partner and this time he was staggering and shouting, much to his lady's embarrassment. Anne remembered a ball, about three years before, when he had staggered around and shouted in just the same way, and it had finished with the police hauling him off home to bed; the next day the headmaster threatened him with the sack. How this memory jarred on her now!

When the samovars in the stalls had cooled down and

the weary ladies of charity had handed over their takings to the old lady with a stone in her mouth, Artynov led Anne by the arm into the ballroom, where supper was being served for the charity bazaar helpers. Twenty of them sat down to supper, no more, but it was all very noisy. His Excellency proposed a toast: 'It would be appropriate, in this luxurious dining-room, to drink to soup kitchens for the poor, which are the object of today's bazaar.' A brigadier proposed a toast to 'that power to which even artillery must surrender' – and all the men clinked glasses with the ladies. It was all very, very lively!

When Anne had been taken home, it was already growing light and cooks were going to market. Very happy, tipsy, brimming with new impressions and quite exhausted, she undressed, collapsed on to her bed and immediately fell asleep.

After one in the afternoon, she was woken up by her chambermaid who announced that Mr Artynov had come to visit her. She quickly dressed, went into the drawing-room, and before long His Excellency arrived to thank her for helping with the charity bazaar. He gave her a sickly look, moved his lips, kissed her hand, asked permission to call again, and left. She stood in the middle of the drawing-room absolutely astonished, enchanted, hardly believing that this change in her life – such an amazing one – had come so quickly. At that moment her husband came in. And now he stood there with the usual grovelling, cloying, servile expression he assumed in the presence of powerful and distinguished people. Convinced that she could say what she liked now, she told him – with rapture, indignation and contempt – 'Clear off, you fathead!', clearly articulating each syllable.

After that, Anne didn't have a single day to herself, since she joined the others for picnics, outings and theatricals. Every day she came back in the early hours, lay down on the drawing-room floor and gave everyone a most touching account of the gay life she was leading. She needed a great deal of money, but she wasn't afraid of Modeste Alekseyevich any more and spent his money as if it were hers. And she didn't even bother to ask for it or demand it, but simply sent him bills or notes saying: 'Pay bearer two hundred roubles' or 'Pay one hundred roubles immediately.'

At Easter, Modeste Alekseyevich was awarded the Order of St Anne, second class. When he called to express his thanks, His Excellency put his paper to one side and sank deeper into his armchair.

'That means you've three Annes now,' he said, examining his white hands and pink nails, 'one in your buttonhole and two round your neck.'

Modeste Alekseyevich pressed two fingers to his lips to stop himself laughing out loud and said, 'Now all I'm waiting for is a little Vladimir.* Dare I ask His Excellency to be the godfather?' He meant the Order of Vladimir,

---

*   Vladimir, also a decoration.

fourth class, and already pictured himself regaling all and sundry with this brilliantly apt and bold pun, and was about to produce another scintillating witticism along the same lines but His Excellency just nodded and plunged into his paper again . . .

Most of the time Anne went riding in a troika, hunting with Artynov, took part in one-act plays, dined out, and visited her family less and less. Peter Leontyevich began to drink more than ever, all his money had gone and they had to sell the harmonium to settle his debts. The boys wouldn't let him out in the street on his own and kept following him in case he fell down. And whenever they met Anne on the Old Kiev Road, riding in a coach and pair with a side horse, Artynov sitting on the box instead of a coachman, Peter Leontyevich would doff his top-hat and start shouting. But then Peter and Andrew would hold him by the arms and plead with him, 'Please stop it, Papa. Please . . .'

COÉDITION ACTES SUD – LEMÉAC

OUVRAGE RÉALISÉ
PAR L'ATELIER GRAPHIQUE ACTES SUD
REPRODUIT ET ACHEVÉ D'IMPRIMER
EN MARS 2013
PAR NORMANDIE ROTO IMPRESSION S.A.S.
À LONRAI
POUR LE COMPTE DES ÉDITIONS
ACTES SUD
LE MÉJAN
PLACE NINA-BERBEROVA
13200 ARLES

DÉPÔT LÉGAL
1ʳᵉ ÉDITION : MAI 2013
Nº impr. : 131213
(Imprimé en France)